# THE WAY HOME

CAROL HOLLAND MARCH

The Way Home
Second Edition
Carol Holland March
Copyright © 2014 Carol Holland March
Published by Compass Rose Press
Albuquerque, New Mexico, USA

"To enter Carol Holland March's imagination is both thrilling and rewarding. Her writing opens up worlds of possibilities."

Lisa Lenard-Cook
Author of *Dissonance* and *Find Your Story, Write Your Memoir*

"*The Way Home* by Carol Holland March includes a novella and eight additional stories in which she writes about relationships in a way that takes us into a special world of energetically charged incidents and seemingly impossible feats. It's the best type of story-fest: in which fantasy crosses into reality and back again. I highly recommend you explore the offerings in *The Way Home*."

Mary Ellen Merrigan, The Merrigan Group

"Carol Holland March, in *The Way Home*, a collection of eight short stories and a novella, harnesses her narrative skill to evoke worlds both familiar and fantastic. Her strong command of language lets her move freely from Chevy trucks bouncing down rutted roads to the immanent realms of legend in which spirit longs to realize itself."

Michael Gray
Author of *Asleep at the Wheel of Time*, *The Flying Caterpillar*, and *Falling on the Bright Side*

"*The Way Home* is an intriguing fantasy collection. Carol Holland March's writing is crisp and elegant, weaving her own magic into each captivating story. From the real world, where there is more than we imagined, to fantasy realms that seem real, Holland March brings a unique perspective sure to delight."

Maer Wilson, Author of the *Modern Magics* series

# TABLE OF CONTENTS

# DESERT SONG

The Chevy truck looked like it had been painted by a team of monkeys on acid. Its front was bright green, the rear a muddy brown, and the camper stuck on its back sported daubs of pink and yellow in no apparent pattern.

"Bought it from a hippie," Ray yelled as he passed the kitchen window. We still said things like that in 1982.

I bolted out the back door in time to see the truck struggle around the corner into what passes for our backyard but looks more like a car cemetery.

The thing looked even worse standing still. The passenger door was hanging on one hinge with a single strand of rope preventing it from peeling off entirely. The windshield was cracked from what appeared to be a bullet hole. It had no front fender and one headlight. When Ray shut off the motor, it kept running for about a minute. I thought it whimpered a couple of times too, but that might have been me. Ray said that he'd gotten it for "almost nothing" which seemed about right.

Ray doesn't get enough auto repairing to suit him at his job at the Ford dealer downtown, so it's not unusual for him to show up with stray vehicles that he fixes up to sell. It brought in extra money, which we needed to survive in San Francisco, even though we lived in a rundown flat in the fog belt a block from Ocean Beach, so close to the zoo we heard the lions roaring at night.

I didn't mind him working on his vehicles on the weekends, but when I saw that truck, I thought he had gone too far. If you'd told me then that I would set out across the western plains in that heap and be chased by a skeleton to boot, I would have called you crazy.

"That's the sorriest-looking vehicle I've ever seen," I told him.

He gave me a hug, crushing me against his chest. "I know it looks bad, Franny, but the engine's sound. I can fix up the camper just like home. You'll see."

I didn't say anything.

"So, are you mad?"

"No. But we're having dinner with Rita and Jake. Their place. Six sharp."

"Aw, Franny. Why don't you let me barbecue up something here?"

"Because we promised."

"Aw, Franny," he said again, but a smile was threatening to break out on his solemn face as he went into the shed to look for the right tool.

2

I left him to it and got going on my errands. As I pointed my Honda north on the coast road, the fog was so heavy you wouldn't have known there was an ocean right there except for the roaring sound the waves made as they broke on Ocean Beach. It was late July, and we hadn't seen the sun for weeks, which didn't bother me like it did Ray.

He's a desert guy from Texas. He had lived all over the southwest and happened to be working a temporary job at the BART repairing subway cars when I met him at a neighborhood bar in East Oakland. I had just hit town and was temping at a law office in Berkeley while I looked for a way to move into the city. He was pretty smitten with me, and would have agreed to just about anything, so I guess I took advantage when I convinced him we could make more money and afford a better place if we crossed the bridge.

It took me a while to figure out he wasn't just being ornery about the fog that hangs over the Outer Sunset much of the year. I thought he would get used to it, that in time the sea would work itself into his soul, and be would be happy living on the edge of the world. Instead, he got quieter. Worked longer hours. Gave me a hard time about things I couldn't help, like mildew in the closets. He shriveled up like an old fig in the sea spray that rusts our cars and makes me feel invincible. It was one of the things we could not reconcile.

Ray worked on the truck the rest of the summer. By Labor Day, it looked better. That weekend he asked me to marry him again, this time trying his luck after we had made love.

"We'll take a trip for our honeymoon," he said, curling himself around my back.

"In that truck? No way. I can't sleep over the cab with the ceiling a couple of inches above my head."

"We don't have to use the cab. The dinette folds out into a bed."

"Sleep in the kitchen?"

"Then we'll fly to Paris. How would that be?"

"I'm afraid to fly."

"So it'll have to be the truck." He kissed the back of my neck. Neither of us mentioned that I hadn't answered his question.

I hated thinking about what we would do with ourselves in the desert for three weeks, but since I wouldn't marry him, have kids, or move to a warmer climate, I was pretty much out of excuses for a road trip. So the day after he finished painting it, in late September, we took off. I was grouchy and tense as we cruised down the interstate toward Los Angeles in the camper now painted turquoise and metallic purple to please me.

It took most of the day to get through the Central Valley—green fields, an occasional barn, flat as Kansas. Ray got lost in the driving, looking as happy as I'd ever

4

seen him, and handsome too in a new plaid shirt, bright green, his sandy brown hair slicked back. His strong hands gripped the steering wheel, and he hummed along with the radio no matter what tune was playing. Every once in a while, he turned to me and curled up the corners of his mouth, like he wanted to tell me something but wasn't sure how to start. I smiled back, determined to say nothing to spoil his mood, and kept on reading the Tony Hillerman novel I'd brought along to get me in the mood for my return to the desert.

As we crossed the Tehachapi Mountains and headed through the Los Padres forest, a full moon rose between two jagged mountain peaks. In Los Angeles, we picked up I-10 going east and soon were doing seventy-five through the suburbs.

That thick, yellow moon was shining its pale light right at me. I asked Ray to pull over so I could look at it from a stationary perspective, but he just looked at me sideways. There were cars all around—four, maybe five lanes—and metal guardrails on the right side instead of a shoulder, so I took his point that stopping to look at the scenery wasn't the best idea I ever had.

"Franny." His fingers closed over my knee. "It's going to be fine. We'll sleep outside tonight if you want."

The tears that had been blocking my throat since we pulled out of the driveway rolled down my face. I was relieved to taste the salt.

"Maybe nothing has changed," I said.

"Is that what has you spooked?"

His blue eyes searched for me in the dark cab.

"You're a grown-up woman now, Franny. What happened back then is long gone. Besides, I'm here now."

I grabbed his hand and squeezed it. He knows why I hate the LA desert, land of my birth, where my mother raised me to go along with whatever came along.

On the night I ran away, fourteen years ago, Ada's face had been pale and angular with orange lips and blue eye shadow. She sat at a metal table in the kitchen of an apartment stinking of fried food and spilled beer. I cowered in a narrow bed, trying not to hear the grunts coming from the next room.

Two days before, the guy I was living with had gotten so high he tried to run me down with his car. The leering yellow lights bore down fast, but I rolled away at the last minute. I ran down the street and straight into a man in a uniform. I collapsed into his arms, sobbing with relief. But the cop knew a crazy woman when he saw one and marched me off to the station. It wasn't until the next evening that Ada got around to coming for me.

She took me to her apartment in west LA where I sat shivering in the tiny bedroom until she and her boyfriend went into the kitchen to eat. Later I went out, thinking he had gone, but he was hunched over the table drinking

6

whiskey out of a dirty glass. He looked at me with dull black eyes and pulled his lips back over big yellow teeth. Knowing that look, I tried to leave, but it was too late.

She made some protest, I remember that, but he was too strong. Did he hit her too? That I don't remember. Only the blows across my head and back until I was quiet for fear his mindlessness would kill me. Afterward he left, slamming the door so hard the walls rattled.

I heard her crying in the other room, drunken sobs that had little to do with me. I cleaned myself up, took the suitcase I hadn't gotten around to unpacking, and got in my car. Drove all the way to Tucson. That was the last time I saw her.

"She's in Albuquerque," I said to Ray, shivering in the warm night air at how clear memories can be. A few letters reached me over the years. Once or twice I wrote back, with no return address. She doesn't know where I live, although my cousin Ruth, who is sworn to secrecy, does. She lives in Albuquerque, where she moved years ago with a guy who was starting a used car business. He disappeared after a couple of months, but she stayed on, getting by on disability for her asthma.

"We aren't going to Albuquerque," Ray said. He stroked my hair. I leaned against his shoulder and watched the moon that was waiting to tell me its secrets.

"We're going to camp tonight?" I asked, suddenly feeling like a child on an outing.

"Under a palm tree."

I thought he was joking, but when he turned off the interstate, we ended up on a dirt road that took us past a row of tall date palms. We dragged our sleeping bags onto a patch of sand and zipped them together. Lying beside him with only our hands touching, I thought about my mother and all the places I had lived. I thought of the men I've been with, good and bad, and how Ray had lasted longer than any of them. Through the swaying branches of the trees, starlight pierced the utter darkness. Ray's hand was warm and solid in mine.

"I love you," Ray said.

I was afraid I'd start crying if I said anything, so I pretended to be asleep. He rolled over and curled his arm around my waist.

In the morning, everything was colored gold, lit by the rising sun. We were in a valley of sand dotted with cactus and scrub bushes with the ungainly palms soaring above us and nothing of civilization in sight. In the distance, desert mountains towered silent and proud; their nakedness held me still for more than a minute. As I walked away from the protection of the trees, the sun seeped into my pores. I felt light and dry, as if I could run all the way to those mountains and all the way back again.

Ray emerged from the camper carrying a coffeepot and two cups. It was a familiar ritual. I sat on a rock and took the cup he offered.

"How you doin'?" he asked.

The lines of worry around his mouth had already softened; sunlight works miracles with Ray. I shook my head. So many words crowded my throat, none came out.

"Did you sleep okay?" he wanted to know.

"Fine. The desert is warming me up."

Something of what I meant must have shown on my face. His eyes crinkled. I placed my untouched coffee on a flat rock. Ray stood and drew me up. I buried my face in his neck and bit the tip of his ear lobe.

I wanted to lie down on that warming sand with the sun in my face and the naked mountains watching over us, and I wanted to feel him reaching for me, all the way inside, as far as anyone has ever got, so my body would beat in time to the vibrations of that place.

After I conveyed this to him with that one hard bite, he muttered into my hair that getting an early start was not always the best plan for the first day of your vacation, and so it was close to ten o'clock before we started east again.

♪♪♪

A couple of days later, when I was thinking this trip maybe hadn't been such a bad idea, the skeleton started following us. We had eaten at a diner in Kingman, Arizona and were driving out of town into the heart of the west. I was mesmerized by the landscape I had seen in a dozen childhood movies when I glanced at the rearview mirror and saw it.

It was running along the sand beside the road, on my side, just far enough behind the truck that I could see it perfectly in the mirror. Its white leg bones were pumping away, its arm bones moving rhythmically as if were a serious long distance runner, minus its flesh and organs.

I snapped my eyes back to the front. We were on old Route 66, a two-lane road that stretched on forever. Huge mountains in the distance. Flat prairie. Rows of hills that I swear were in some movie where Indians watched a wagon train of settlers go by. I glanced sideways at Ray to see if he had noticed anything. He was humming under his breath. He felt my eyes and turned.

"How you doin?" he asked.

"Great," I said.

He winked and turned back to the road.

I looked back at the side mirror. The skeleton lifted its spindly white right arm and waved.

The tide inside me was rising, from deep in my belly all the way into my throat. Leave it to me to come to the desert to drown, I thought wildly. With a few deep breaths, I pushed it down and threw a couple of logs of driftwood at it. The tide surged against the logjam, groaned twice, and receded. I stared straight ahead.

10

By the time we got to Seligman, a little prairie town that looked like the modern world had moved on without it, the familiar pain in my back had started throbbing. There was no medical reason for it. I had been checked. It started when I was a teen-ager, with monthly lower back pain like a lot of women get. But as time when on, it wormed its way deeper, into nerves and vital organs, twisting its way up my spinal cord and attacking my lungs, shoulders, and finally penetrating my neck. When that happened, I couldn't move my head to either side. It was like being sucked dry by a creature with tentacles. It reminded me of the horror movies about aliens from outer space.

Those movies never scared me. I didn't see much difference between slimy aliens with evil intent and what I was already hauling around. At least you'd get some sympathy if you took off your coat and showed somebody a fishy tail hanging out of your back. On bad days I could feel the thing slithering around my lungs, going for my heart, squeezing until I could hardly breathe. Then my back would spasm. In protest, I thought at first, but no, the thing had its roots in there, deep in the big muscles in my hips. The spasms were its victory dance.

As long as I could remember, I knew I was doing something wrong. Didn't matter what it was. Got a job. Quit the job. Moved to a different town. Found a lover. Went to school. You name it.

Nothing was right, and the thing inside me was quick to point it out, with all its squeezing and thrashing around. The only way to beat it was to keep perfectly still, the one thing I refused to do. After I met Ray, the pain didn't come as often. My body knew, even if the rest of me didn't.

"Are you okay?" he asked.

I was practicing not telling lies, not even little ones.

"I don't know," I said, settling. "My back hurts."

"Could be the desert," he said as if it were perfectly natural. "Want to lie down in the back?"

Lying down felt worse than sitting, so I folded my arms over my belly, wishing I had another pair of arms to hold the place behind my heart. Ray would have done it if I asked. He liked to rub between my shoulder blades in slow clockwise circles, but I felt too tender for touching, so I hunched over and willed the muscles in my back to relax on their own. Ray kept driving.

The skeleton stuck with us as we crossed the mountains at Flagstaff where it was cool and green. I thought a more populated area might scare it off, but it kept running along the right side of the road, at a pace to keep it the same distance behind us. When we drove through town, it moved onto the shoulder. When we came down the other side of San Francisco Peak into the canyon lands, the skeleton moved off the asphalt and

12

back onto the desert. I got the impression it enjoyed running on sand.

The pain in my back felt like somebody was using a blowtorch on me. The heat snaked behind my heart, through my chest, and scorched my arms. By the time we got to Winslow, I was in flames.

"Do you want to stop?" Ray asked. "You haven't eaten all day."

The last thing I wanted was to encounter strangers. "No," I said. We were sitting at a crossroads with emptiness all around us. "Why don't you go left here?"

He looked at me. "Why left?"

"When in doubt, always go left," I said, trying to sound adventurous. "Maybe we'll find a place to have a picnic."

Ray shrugged and turned down a narrow road that wound around dry hills. After a while, we came to a stand of cottonwoods by a little stream.

"Stop here," I said. I didn't know what was going to happen, but it felt right. I got out of the truck, and pretended this was the place we had been driving for days to get to. I asked Ray to get some food out of the camper and went to sit under a cottonwood. I noticed it was whispering excitedly to its neighbors that they had company at last. I hadn't seen the skeleton since we turned off the main road, but I wasn't optimistic about that.

I ate the soup and bread that Ray brought, but I couldn't sit there for long. I told him I needed privacy, ignored how his face tightened up, and set off walking down the bank of the little stream. At a grassy place under another cottonwood that looked inviting, I lay down on the bank and let one hand drift through the water. The current brushed against my skin. I looked up through the old tree's branches at the perfect blue sky and tried to figure out what to do.

It came to me to roll, so I started doing that. As I gathered momentum, I felt like moaning, so I did some of that too. The pain was so intense I wasn't sure I'd ever get up again, but I kept on rolling around in the grass, feeling the friction against my arms and legs and moaning to beat the band. The flames inside me died to embers.

I thought about this thing inside me that was trying to get out. It would be something soft and slimy, maybe with scales. It might take all my organs with it, so this golden tree and azure sky could be the last things I ever saw. I moaned about that. My only regret was Ray. But what good was I to him like this?

A sharp pain attacked my tailbone, as if someone had slit me open with a knife. I stuffed my fist against my mouth so I wouldn't scream. Then it slid out of me. A thick stream of black viscous liquid. It pooled on the grass and soaked into the sandy soil. As it poured out, the pain dissolved. The black liquid kept coming, with no blood or guts that I could see. No body parts wiggled in the sand. I could feel it releasing my heart and lungs. It moved down my spine and out the back until there was nothing left. I turned onto my side and watched the sand absorb the black gunk.

I used the trunk of the tree to pull myself up and walked back to where we had parked. Ray was busy digging a substantial hole with the shovel he kept in the camper.

"What are you doing?" I asked.

He nodded to his right. The skeleton was partially buried in the sand, lying on its back with its hands folded over its pelvis. Weeds poked through its ribs.

"Found it there after you went for your walk," he said. "I don't like the idea of it lying in the open like that."

He sounded so serious, like this was an ordinary problem, that I started to laugh. I laughed so hard I had to sit down.

The afternoon was fading and the desert light coalescing into that deep focus that lets you see more than you can at noon. I looked hard at that skeleton. For just a moment, I swore I saw Ada's face on it, gaunt and saggy and sad.

When Ray finished with the grave, I helped him place the skeleton on a blanket. I was afraid it would disintegrate into a heap as we lifted it, but it kept its shape perfectly. We lowered it down. Tears came into my eyes as I looked at it lying so helpless in that hole, but for the first time in my life, I was sure I was doing the right thing.

While I pushed the dirt Ray had excavated back into the grave, Ray wandered around picking up stones. I told him to never mind, that no one would ever want to find the place again, but he said it was only right. He heaped up a pretty good pile of rocks.

"It looks funny," I said when he was done.

"Really out of place," he agreed.

He pulled me against his chest. "There's a little canyon just up this road. Let's drive up and watch the night come on."

When we got to the canyon rim, I asked him how he knew about this place.

"Saw the road go up the hill. Come on, the colors in the rocks are turning."

And they were. I stood on the rim of the canyon, with the creek a couple of hundred feet below us and the sun setting everything ablaze in pinks and golds and metallic browns, and the green of junipers clinging to vertical cliffs. Just as if I were cut loose from my body, I knew what it would be like to fall over the edge, to spiral down as slow and easy as a hawk, past the desert rocks and colored sand to the creek below. I grabbed Ray's arm.

16

"Look," he said. He bent and picked up a tiny seashell.

"How did that get here?"

"This was once a seabed."

In my mind, I saw it, the great flood of receding water, the plains appearing, the shelled creatures abandoned on mountaintops. The backed-up tide inside me broke through the last of my carefully erected barriers. Tears poured out of me, spilling down my face and onto my shirt.

The sun disappeared, setting us all ablaze in a final burst of light.

"Ray."

He looked down.

"I've never stayed in one place as long as I have with you."

"Franny," he said.

I could have gotten away with just that. I could have said almost anything next and he would have been satisfied. But in the midst of all that clear, hard beauty, I couldn't play the coward.

"I'm scared," I said. "Scared to depend on anybody. Scared to let myself open up the way you deserve. Scared I'll end up trapped and hateful without any way out."

"That's what you think will happen to us?" The pain in his voice tore at my chest. A cottony feeling in my mouth stopped me from answering so I just leaned against him, listening to his heartbeat.

"If you wanted to go, I wouldn't stop you." He sounded like he was being strangled. "I love you so much, sometimes I think it's going to be the death of me, if the fog doesn't get me first, but I'd never hold you back."

"What if I'm not what you think?"

"I know what you are."

"You do?"

He nodded. "You gotta stop running sometime. If you don't want to move, we'll stay in the city. If you don't want kids, that's all right. If you don't love me, then be straight with me. But if you do, give us a chance to figure it out."

Night was falling. The air brushed cool against my face. A crow screeched overhead. And something else. I heard music, low and deep, coming from way below my feet. It rippled through me and out my head, echoing over the canyons and plains.

"Do you hear that?" I asked.

"Sure," he answered. "Every place has a song."

I looked at him and all of a sudden it hit me. Water or sand, it didn't matter. This is where I was supposed to be. We watched the stars come out.

Finally, I said, "This is where I stopped. Maybe we should erect a monument."

The moon had risen. In its light, Ray's smile started with a twitch at the corners of his mouth. It spread over his face until his eyes crinkled up the way they do when he's tickled.

He leaned down and kissed me. I snuggled up close to him so together we could feel the warmth of that big yellow moon smiling down on us.

∞

# THE CALL OF THE BENU

"You have the best shoulder," his lover said. She crept closer and pushed her head against his neck.

"Hush," he said, stroking her jutting hipbone.

She wrapped a cold leg around his warm one. "Sometimes I want to talk."

"Let the medicine work."

She sighed. "I've always loved you. From the beginning of time."

She always said that, and he had never believed her. Now he wanted to.

She whimpered in her sleep. He stroked her pale hair, cut short and dry as straw, as he lay awake, staring into the darkness, listening to her breathe. Toward morning, the sound of distant gunfire woke him.

∫∫∫

She rose slowly, on unsteady feet. She had been asleep for a long time. Her wings ached as she stretched them, but

20

when they were extended and the air ruffled the feathers on her wingtips, she remembered the joy of flight, and raised her long neck into the breeze. Flapping the great wings, she lifted into the air. She was very hungry. She made for the shallows along the coast where small fish were easy to find. Soon it would be time to go, but first she would eat.

ʃʃʃ

In the morning, she was too tired to get up. He brought her tea and the last of the bread. "We need food," he said. "No one's left, so I'm going to try the houses on the next street." He didn't mention that he had given her the last of the sleeping pills.

"Where have they gone?"

He sat on the bed and held her hand. "The town's been evacuated. They've gone south."

"What happened?" she asked, as if he had never mentioned it before.

"The war. Bombs were dropped in the north. If they find us, they could separate us."

"I won't make a sound."

He kissed her and went out to search for canned goods in their neighbors' kitchens. When he returned, she was sitting at the window facing the bay, watching puffs of smoke swirling above the mainland.

"We're safe here," she said as he heated soup on a propane camp stove. "It's an island."

"Drink your soup. They won't find us if we don't use the lights."

She lifted the cup to her mouth but did not drink. "I remember Egypt. It was hot and dry and you were more beautiful than anyone I'd ever seen. When you touched me, I knew I would never leave you."

He ate his beans cold, from the can. He had heard all her stories of their past lives, but she had settled on Egypt. Maybe because she was always cold. When she finished the soup, he took the cup and placed it on the table. He plumped her pillows and eased her back in bed. She was still beautiful, with her high cheekbones and wide eyes. Now they were cavernous, doors into places he could not go. He pulled the blankets up to her chin. "Try to sleep."

"She's coming."

"Who is?"

"You'll see. Egypt is right here." She motioned with a thin, white hand at empty space.

"All right."

She turned and looked into the empty space. "Maybe it isn't Egypt. It doesn't matter. It's beautiful. And warm. But we have to wait for her."

"All right," he said. "But try to sleep. Save your strength."

She looked up at him and compressed her lips. "You have to promise that you'll do what I ask. When the time comes."

"I'm doing what I can."

She touched his face. "I know. Promise me anyway."

"I promise," he said helplessly.

∫∫∫

Fish were plentiful in the shallows. She stood like a statue until they swam close, and then stabbed them with her long, pointed bill. She swallowed them whole. She ate until her strength returned. When she pointed her bill toward the sky, it was no longer blue. Gray and angry. No sun to warm her feathers. It was time.

She opened her wings wide. With a single leap, she was airborne. She released a wild cry of pleasure and flew straight up. Gray clouds and smoke. Cinders in the air. She settled into a slow, rhythmic pumping, her wings level with her long body. She flew over water, because that was her home, but kept the coastline in sight. It would tell her when she had arrived.

∫∫∫

He watched the helicopter fly up and down the coastline, searching for survivors. A disembodied voice echoed from what was probably a megaphone on a jeep. It didn't pass the house, but it was close. It advised them to come out so they could be taken to a safe place. It was their last chance. He bit his lip and stayed far from the window.

"What's wrong?" she said, waking.

"Nothing. They want us to leave."

She shook her head. "It won't be long now."

He held her icy hand. "Probably not. Are you hungry?"

"No. I was dreaming of Egypt again. I can still see it." She motioned to the empty space between them. "It has a beach. Like ours, but better. Pure white sand. Crystal rocks. Pools of warm water under waterfalls. We'll sit all day in the sunshine, and healers will come to help us. I'll be well again."

He kissed her. "It sounds wonderful."

She stroked his brown arm with her pure white fingers. "You're worried."

"A little." He could never lie to her.

"The only hard part will be getting to the beach. I don't know if I can walk."

He looked out the window toward the bay. Only a block away. If that's where she wanted to go, it wasn't impossible. "I'll carry you."

"Do you know the big rock?" she asked. "The signal rock, we called it when we were kids."

He knew it. It was on the ocean side of the island. It towered above the beach a hundred yards from shore. "It's a long way. I'll take you to the beach along the bay instead. We always swam there."

She opened her dark eyes wider and looked all the way into him. "I know you're worried, but I have to go to signal rock. Promise me."

"If they see us, they won't let us stay here."

"They're leaving," she said.

She was right. The next day, the helicopter was gone. There was no sound except for the screeching gulls and the wind moving through the tired joints of the old house.

♫♫♫

She stroked steadily, rhythmically, the land to her left, open sea to her right. She gained strength as she flew. Joy moved through her body, warming her with every wing stroke. She lived for endings and beginnings. The time was coming, and she would be its instrument.

♫♫♫

He woke slowly and only gradually realized that he held feathers in his arms. A warm, pulsing heart beat against his chest, so fast it frightened him. Something curved around the top of his head, heavy and soft. He opened his eyes and saw the blue-feathered body under his hands, the long yellow bill resting against his side. He opened his mouth to scream, and woke again. She was there, curled against him in her familiar shape.

His movements roused her. "What is it?"

"Nothing. A dream."

"What did you dream?"

"That you were a bird. As big as a person."

In the moonlight from the window, she smiled. "Tomorrow we'll go to the beach."

"It's too dangerous."

"You promised."

"Yes," he said, and held her tighter.

ʃʃʃ

He walked a mile through deserted streets to the drugstore. Even in this close-knit seaside town, there had been looting. He picked his way through discarded merchandise and found plastic bottles of water and over-the-counter sleeping aids to stuff in his backpack. Behind the pharmacist's counter, the contents of boxes and drawers were strewn on the floor. He picked through them methodically until he found a container of pain killers, and then another. He took some brightly colored boxes of cold remedies and cough syrup, stuffed them into the pack and hoisted it onto his shoulders.

When he returned to the house, she was dressed in her old jeans and one of his sweaters. She smiled at him with a trace of the old light in her eyes.

"We have to go," she said. "Is there gas in the car?"

He let the pack slide to the floor. "We used the last of it." He pulled out the bottles of water and boxes of medicine and piled them on the bureau.

"Bring the water."

His heart lifted at her decisive tone. She hadn't had such a good day in weeks.

"I dreamed about the healing pools in Egypt again. But we need gas so we can get to the beach."

He looked out the window. The street below was littered with abandoned cars. It felt odd to take a car that had belonged to a neighbor, but he was sure they were the last people left. "I'll look for a car with gas. He picked up a bottle from the bureau. "I found tramadol. It's an opiate." He handed it to her.

She tucked it into the pocket of her jeans. "Maybe later. Find a car. I love you."

"El," he said, and stopped. Nothing he could say would make a difference. What would be gained by driving to the beach he couldn't fathom, but she was clearly stronger, and so he would take her. For an hour, he swore. No longer. "I'll find a car. It's cold outside. Wait here and I'll come up. You need a coat. And hat."

She hugged his waist. "I know how hard this is." He wondered if they were talking about the same thing. It was never easy to tell. "I'll wait," she said and motioned him out the door.

He went to three cars before he found one with a key, but it wouldn't start. The next two were locked. Then he saw the old van. A relic, painted pink and gray. The key was under the mat. It started on the third try. The red needle registered a quarter of a tank, more than enough. He put it in first and eased it away from the curb and around the block. He was surprised when a stream of warm air issued from the vents at his feet.

He parked it in the middle of the street under her window. He ran up the stairs and found her sitting on the bed, wearing her down coat, a scarf wrapped three times around her neck, and a red wool hat. He held out his hand. "Come look." He guided her to the window and pointed down at the van.

She laughed and hugged him. "I love it. It's like the one I had in college, when I went to visit you in Maine. Do you remember that weekend?"

He pulled two blankets from the bed and draped them around her shoulders. He didn't remember the van, but he remembered her appearing suddenly one night, her golden hair falling to her waist, her huge eyes looking only at him. They made love for the first time, crushed into his narrow cot in the attic room of a drafty house on the coast. She had reached up and touched the slanted beams with her long fingernails while he buried himself in her.

"Of course I remember," he said. "Until then I thought you'd never noticed me."

She kissed his cheek. Her lips were dry. "I always noticed you. Since Egypt, you've never been out of my mind for long."

He arranged the blankets around her until she looked like a misshapen toy with a red top. "It has heat. We'll go to the beach, but we can't stay long. It's too cold."

She pushed her face out of the blankets. "It's the end of the world. Time has stopped. You should believe me."

He kissed her nose. "I believe you." He pulled on his heavier jacket, and slipped on the backpack stuffed with water and extra pain pills, half a loaf of rye bread, and a packet of processed cheese.

♫♫♫

The beach was gray and deserted. A cold wind blew from the sea, forming whitecaps all the way to the horizon. He drove to the end of the pavement and parked. They walked on a path through the dunes, his arm around her shoulders.

"I want to go to the water's edge." Her voice was breathless and excited.

He picked her up and staggered down to the hard-packed sand left by the outgoing tide. He spread out one of the blankets, and they sat wrapped in the other one, facing the sea and signal rock, which looked higher and more forbidding than he remembered. The wind died as they huddled against each other. She pressed her face against his shoulder and smiled, her eyes bright.

"I wouldn't have made it without you," she said. "Not this far. I owe you everything."

He thought she had it backwards, but he just squeezed her arm. "What's going to happen now?"

"I know you don't believe me, but you'll see. When she gets here, she'll open the door. It's our next place, Addie."

Tears scratched at his eyes. "Where is it, El? This place?"

"I never know," she said dreamily. "I go there in my dreams, but I can't tell where it is. Maybe it is Egypt. But look." She motioned toward the ruined town. "There's nothing left here. There's nothing to lose, is there?"

He kissed her red hat. "Not really, no. Are you cold?"

"A little. Did you bring the water?"

He had left the pack in the car so he could carry her. "I'll get it. I'll bring some driftwood and make a fire. Is that all right?"

Her eyes shone. "I'd love a fire."

He eased her down on the blanket and wrapped the second one around her. "Rest until I get back, okay? Do you want your pills?"

She shook her head. "I want to be awake."

He started back across the sand toward the van, glad to be away from her, because he could no longer stop the tears from spilling down his face.

♪♪♪

As she passed the barrier islands, she flew faster. Gulls circled below her, but not as many as there should have been. She looked into the sea and, even there, saw only the occasional seal and no dolphins.

She sought a sign to tell her that she had arrived at the place of appointment. She did not know what it was, but it would reveal itself. The smoke from afar was thick, unsettling. Strange, staccato noises came from the mainland. She had slept too long, but it was not in her nature to berate herself. She was here now, and very close.

When she saw the black rock rising out of the sea, something shifted in her breast. She aimed for it. As she approached, she saw several places below its pointed peak where she could land. She flew in a wide circle, over the beach, over the sand dunes dotted with bright dune grass, over the edge of the populated portion of the island.

A single human figure held sticks of wood in its arms. She flew around again, over the sea, around the rock, back toward the beach. This time, a woman stood alone by the water's edge, one arm raised in greeting. There was always a lone woman on the beach to greet her. She remembered. That was the sign.

She flew lower over the black rock, stretched out her long legs, and landed on a narrow ledge. She settled her wings against her body and raised her head. She shook herself and tucked her head under a wing. Sunset was the time. She would sleep until then. The wind ruffled her feathers as she dreamed of a human hand, slowly stroking her back.

∫∫∫

When he returned with the driftwood, El was standing by the water's edge, her blanket forgotten. He dumped the wood in a pile and picked up the blanket. "Here," he said, putting it around her shoulders. "You need to stay warm."

She faced him with shining eyes and color in her face. "She's here. On the rock. She saw me."

He finished wrapping her up and looked toward the rock. More than anything he could imagine, he wanted to know what had come for her. "I don't see anything."

She lifted her face for a kiss. "Just wait." She knelt on the blanket while he built the fire. The wood was dry. Soon they were warming their hands in the glow from the flames. He opened the backpack and brought out the water and food. He spread cheese on a slice of bread and handed it to her. She toasted him with her water bottle. They ate while the tide ebbed and the fire burned.

She snuggled against him and sipped at her water. "It will happen at sunset."

He looked around. He could almost pretend everything was normal. An empty beach. Waves crashing. Gulls pecking at clamshells.

"I don't want to lose you," he said. "But you're right. There's nothing here for us."

In his back pocket was a penknife with a very sharp blade. He noticed he was thinking that opening a vein might not be the worst way to go. When the time came. "I love you, El. I've loved every day we've been together."

She pushed herself against him. "I know," she whispered. "And it isn't over."

At that moment, the tide stood still.

The great bird raised her head. She opened her wings and stretched them wide. The sun appeared on the horizon, emerging from behind a mass of dark clouds. The light reflected on the bird's wings, so they shone golden red in the dying light.

He looked up. As the bird leaped into the air, the enormous red wings spread out, making the creature look so large it seemed like a phantasm from another world. "Oh, God," he breathed.

El smiled. "Help me up. I need to be standing."

He rose and pulled her up with him. Together they watched the bird circle the rock, her wings now bluish gray. She circled twice and landed on the beach at the water's edge.

"Is this what you expected?"

She nodded. She shrugged off the blanket and removed the red hat. "Stay here, Addie, I have to do something."

He reached for her, but she had started toward the bird, now motionless on legs as long as stilts. The long yellow bill moved up and down, the bright green eyes shone.

El stopped in front of the bird taller than she was. Its head lowered. The bill rested, first on one of her shoulders, then the other. El reached out and gently stroked the soft blue feathers. "It's been a long time."

The bird lowered its head so she could stroke the two long narrow feathers, dark as indigo, protruding from its crest. When it raised its head, El walked back to Addie. "Thank you for bringing me, even though you didn't believe."

He was still staring at the enormous bird. What do I believe? he thought wildly. Have I died? Did we both die in a bomb strike and this is all a crazy dream?

She looped her arm around his waist. "Listen."

He listened to the wind, the waves, to the cries of gulls, and to the sound the wings of the great bird made as it lifted from the beach and flew around the black rock. He listened as it landed on the very tip of the rock, and as it opened its beak and emitted the cry that has been heard a thousand times by those graced to perceive the call into existence of a new world.

When the call thundered, he clapped his hands to his ears. He turned to the woman he had loved for fifteen years. Her smile was as bright as the sun perched on the horizon. It was the first time in weeks they had seen it. He turned again to look at the bird, but it had disappeared into its own call.

El started to say to Addie that everything was all right now, but he was already moving toward the sea.

His eyes were wide and soft, his lips parted in a half-smile. He held fast to her hand and pulled her behind him as he strode into the bright light that had appeared where the bird had stood.

She giggled as she had when she was a girl, and tossed her short hair exactly as she used to do when it hung to her waist. She squeezed his fingers hard and ran a few steps to catch up. Side by side, they walked into the tunnel of light.

Neither of them looked back.

# DREAMING
# IN AND OUT

The darkness whispers in my ears as I stumble through a labyrinth of tunnels, a stone maze with rough walls as sharp as glass, curving one way, then the other. Too dark even for shadows.

I stumble on, my right hand trailing the rough rock, my left extended straight ahead. I crash against something hard and fall to my knees. Pain slices through my right leg. I smell blood. I don't want to think about what might be crawling in the darkness. I get up and stagger forward.

Light appears. The wall of the tunnel curves to the left. I move faster, crawl under a rocky ledge, and come to an arch that leads into an open area. Light shines from an opening above—too high to reach—but enough to see by. I stand and wait for my eyes to adjust. A circular room, shadowed edges. An open pit in the center, full of white ashes. Around it a low wall, no more than a foot high, a circle of stones surrounding the pit.

From the far side of the room something moves. A flash of white. Out of the shadows a woman steps forward, moves toward the circle. She wears a long white dress — plain, cotton, pure. She has red hair like mine but longer. She is older, with haunted eyes. I want to speak but my throat constricts.

I flatten myself too hard against the wall of the cave. A sharp rock tears the thin material of my shirt and punctures the skin behind my heart. She walks toward the wall of stone, steps over it, and kneels in the ashes. She looks straight at me as she slowly lowers the straps of her white dress to reveal the red gash where her left breast had been.

## ∫∫∫

He wakes me with rough fingers pinching my nipples so hard it hurts. His body is heavy against my back, hard and sweaty. I try to roll away from him, but there is no room left on the bed.

"Stop," I say.

His right arm is under my shoulders. With that hand he pinches me harder. His left hand moves down between my legs. I am not ready but he pushes into me anyway. To get away, I roll onto the floor, get up, and look back at him. He grins. He thinks this is a game.

"I have to go to work," I say.

"C'mon," he says. "It won't take long."

I go into the bathroom to shower.

On the bus into town I remember the woman in white. A shiver moves up my spine and through the back of my head. My ears pulse. It is not the first time I have dreamed of her.

ʃʃʃ

Again, the labyrinth. My forehead throbs in rhythm with my breath. Pitch dark all around. No way to go but forward and pray not to fall into a pit that will disintegrate my flesh.

When I see the light in the distance, I want to turn and run, but the light wins. Perhaps the mutilated woman will show me the way to the surface. I duck under the ledge. See the pit. The wall. She walks out of the shadows, slowly, as if walking onto a stage where she will deliver the speech of her life. She steps across the wall. Kneels in the pile of white ash. Looks straight at me. I cringe against the wall of lava rock.

She lowers her dress. Both breasts are gone. I stare at the red gashes on her chest, uneven blue lines where crude stitches hold her together. She raises her arms above her head. Her colorless mouth forms into a sweet smile that makes me want to scream.

"I waited for the Lord of Time," she says in a voice like an echo in a cathedral long deserted by the gods of man.

I wake sweating. His hand is cupped around my left breast, his whiskey breath against my hair. What does he dream about? I wonder, as I untangle myself and go to watch the sun rise over the mountains from the window in the kitchen.

∫∫∫

In the park I sit on a bench to watch the other women with their children. A little girl runs after her yellow ball that has rolled close to my feet. I reach down and pick up the round plastic thing. It feels light and hopeful. We look at each other. She holds out her small hands. I throw the ball to her. She catches it but does not turn away. "Thank you," she says in a solemn voice as if she has been taught to be polite to strangers. "Do you want to play?"

"I don't know how," I say. I see her mother approaching, concerned about the strange woman talking to her daughter.

"You throw it," the child says. She throws me the ball. I catch it and throw it back.

"Come along, Emily," says her mother. Something about me has warned her.

The child smiles and turns away. Over Emily's head, I look at her mother. I do not smile. She is right to be wary.

40

I sit on the bench long after Emily and her mother have gone. People come and go. They play with their dogs and their children. They seem happy. I wonder how far I could get on the two hundred and twenty-two dollars I have secreted in the back of the bedroom closet, in the false bottom of a box filled with mismatched buttons.

He brought me to this city a year ago, for a better job, he said, but it was to remove me from everything familiar. My sister Susan is two thousand miles away. I have no friends. Only on the one day when he works and I don't can I come to the park and pretend I am not a prisoner.

"You're crazy," Susan said when I told her I was leaving with him. "He doesn't love you. It's something else."

Now that I know she was right, it's too late. I wonder if Emily's mother is loved. I wonder if I will survive long enough to tell Susan she was right and that I will never leave home again. I wonder who the Lord of Time could be.

♪♪♪

Darkness again. I bang my shins against the lava rocks, but I must hurry through the labyrinth. A cobweb catches my face. I brush at it furiously and go on. It seems a longer journey this time, more turns, different directions. I fear being lost and stop to pant. I quiet myself. The darkness around me grays. I can almost see the way. I must find her. I go on and after two more turns, find the lighted archway. She is in the center of the circle, kneeling, head bowed to the ashes. The white dress is red-stained.

She raises her head and looks at me with eyes so huge her horror is reflected in them. I am frozen, but she struggles to her feet, using only her right hand to balance herself. Her left hand is hidden in the folds of her stained dress. Standing, she picks at her hair, as if to make herself presentable. She presses down on her skirt.

*What has happened?* I think to her.

Slowly—so slowly—she moves her left arm out of the folds of her skirt. Her arm drips. Her hand has been ripped off at the wrist. She wipes the blood on her skirt and averts her eyes.

"I waited too long," she whispers. The sound reverberates around the gray stone walls as if she had shouted them again and again.

*What did you wait for?*

Two tears roll down her white face. "Eternity," she says.

∫∫∫

He comes home late and screams at me because the meatloaf is dry.

"I'm sorry," I say and hate myself for cringing. I smell beer on his breath and understand to lower my eyes when I answer.

"You're useless," he sneers. "You can't cook. All you're good for is fucking."

"Let me go." I am suddenly brave. "You can find someone better."

He pushes me against the stove. My head hits the wall where the clock ticks off the hours. "Don't even think about it," he sneers against my throat. "If you leave, I'll find you. I'll find you and slice you up like a cow. Do you hear me, Jen? Jennifer?" He mocks me with my own name.

I nod and try not to breathe.

He releases me. When I stand up, he pushes me toward the bedroom. I think about grabbing a knife from the drawer and gutting him before he can take another step. I think about his blood pooling on the dingy white tiles. About watching him die. How his face would contort in disbelief. How his eyes would dim. About telling the police, who would invade the apartment with their uniforms and nightsticks, their red faces, thick hands poised over their guns.

He pushes me onto the bed and presses my face into a pillow so I will not cry out.

♪♪♪

43

The cave is not so dark this time. Do I remember seeing this rock outcropping? Have I learned the way? Or does my dream-self perceive momentum where there is only repetition?

This time I do not fall. When I come to the archway, she waits, silent and still in the shadows. She steps over the wall. Kneels in the ashes. The blood has stopped dripping.

Who is the Lord of Time? I ask.

She smiles. Awkwardly, with one hand, she pushes herself up and stands erect.

I move toward her. I go as far as the wall and stop.

"He comes," she says.

Something moves in the shadows. She shrinks back, steps over the wall and out of the circle of ashes. From the shadows a swirling figure glides. I step back.

It enters the circle and dances, its legs moving so quickly I cannot see them clearly. Its arms—so many arms—in synchronized measured moves, fly up and down, swing sideways in a kinesis that is clearly language, one I cannot speak. His matted hair swings in rhythm with his sinuous body as he crouches and leaps and bends. Around the stone wall, a huge multi-colored snake winds itself.

I am mesmerized by the dancing. I glance at the woman in white, who is backed against the stone wall to my left. "It is an image," she says. "Too old to be useful."

The dancer shimmers and fades. It recomposes itself into a comic book devil with a long, thin tail and tiny black horns. Perfect for Halloween.

She laughs. I join her, and the image devolves into smoke. Out of the smoke a huge, shining angel takes shape. It is pale and translucent, with wings that stretch as far as the cave walls and a face so bright I turn away.

This one stops my laughter, but the woman in white shrugs. "Eternity cannot be won," she says. The angel evaporates into a pool of white dust that settles into the ashes.

A dusty cloud moves into the corner of my vision. I look directly at it. From the pale dust, a child rises. A boy, perhaps five years old, wearing a three-piece tan suit with a yellow handkerchief in the pocket. He is dark-haired with bright green eyes. He comes toward me and offers me a bouquet of yellow roses. I kneel to accept them. I look into his eyes.

"Eternity is what you do," he says.

I take the roses and breathe in their scent. In their midst is a plastic handle. I pull it out. It is a hairbrush.

"Open it," he says.

I pull out the stiletto dagger concealed within the handle.

I wake suddenly, heart pounding.

He is snoring beside me. I go into the bathroom. In the mirror, I look the same. Haggard. Old beyond my years.

On the sink is a different hairbrush than the one I use every morning. It fits my hand perfectly. I do not tremble. I take the hairbrush in my left hand and pull with my right. The knife slides out. I stand there and balance the stiletto in my palm. I grip it and practice slashing down. Then I grip it another way and practice slashing forward.

As I walk back into the bedroom, I am strangely calm. The knife in my hand is hypnotic. It is so early, he is still drunk, not likely to awaken. I stand over him. I think of Susan. I think of the woman in white. I think of the little boy with green eyes.

♫♫♫

I dress quickly, in jeans and shirt, sweater and jacket, as if I am going somewhere farther than the park. I put on boots even though it is warm enough for shoes. I retrieve my box of buttons and stuff the bills I have saved into the back pocket of my jeans. I put the box back in exactly the same place. I shove my purse into the backpack I got for the camping trips we never took and lock the door behind me.

I sit on my favorite bench. People come and go. At lunch time the park is crowded with children and dogs. Emily and her mother come. Emily carries her yellow ball. I watch while a little boy in a tan suit approaches her. They toss the ball back and forth, giggling endlessly.

46

When the game is over, all three walk past me. The little boy comes to my side as if he knows me. Emily's mother thinks he is my child. She smiles. I smile back.

He is close enough to touch. When he looks up at me, my heart pounds. "It's almost time," he says.

I feel as though I am melting into the wooden bench.

∫∫∫

She appeared as the light was fading. I thought she was old, but as she came closer, I saw she was near my age, but ragged and tired. She pushed a shopping cart filled with her belongings along the winding cement path. She wore a white dress, yellow with age and stained down the front, under a short blue jacket at least two sizes too large. When she came to my bench, she stopped and raised her eyebrows as if asking a question I had promised long ago to answer.

I pulled out my purse and offered her a five dollar bill. She looked at it for a long moment before she accepted it with a chapped, red hand.

"For passage," she said. "If you're ready."

I wasn't sure what I was ready for, but I picked up my backpack and followed her through the park. We walked down the street that led to the river which ran through the city and, eventually, to the sea. The river was lined with a grassy area and old trees and walking trails with benches, so older people could rest in the shade with their dogs.

She led me to a small wooden dock where four rowboats were moored. They bobbed gently in the green water. The small building advertising "Boats for rent" was locked, the proprietor gone for the day.

We sat together on a bench at the water's edge and watched a mother duck lead six ducklings downstream. Their tiny yellow feet paddled through the water just as they were born to do.

I watched the setting sun turn the green water golden, a few purple irises blooming on the shore. I thought about the garden behind Susan's house and wondered if the tulips had come up.

I looked at the woman. She nodded as if she knew what I wanted to ask her.

"Time can be bent," she said, still without turning toward me. "But you do need a boat."

I pulled the rest of the bills from my pocket and tried to give them to her, but she shook her head.

"You have farther to go," she said. "You might need them."

"Thank you," I said.

"You had better start."

I was dubious about rowing, but I dropped my pack into the bottom of the nearest boat. I stepped in and fitted the oars into the oarlocks. I looked back at the woman sitting on the bench. "Who are you?" I asked her.

She smiled then and shrugged once, as a grandmother might. I untied the single rope. The boat floated away from the dock.

The rowing wasn't as hard as I had imagined. The little boat went downstream at a surprising clip. I turned around and waved. She waved back. The current took me. I knew it would not be a straight trip across the river. I also knew I would land at the place where I was intended to go.

Even so, I looked back again and again, until my boat rounded the first curve of land and I could no longer see her sitting there as I rowed away in the deepening dusk toward the opposite shore.

∞

# THE CONVERSATION

*"The most beguiling moment in the hunt is the first moment of the encounter. Wolves and prey may remain absolutely still while staring at each other. I think what transpires in those moments is an exchange of information between predator and prey that either triggers a chase or defuses the hunt right there. I call this exchange the conversation of death…"*

Barry Lopez, "On Wolves and Men"

It appeared from nowhere and sat down in the front yard, just inside the wooden gate hanging on one hinge. Terry was cleaning out the detritus of a lifetime from her mother's house. When she opened the front door, she saw it.

She tossed another bag on the mound of black plastic bags piled by the fence and stopped to wipe the sweat from her eyes. The landscape shimmered. All shades of brown. A few spots of yellow rabbitbrush amidst the washed-out creosote and mesquite. No houses for a mile. Mountains in the distance. Early September, but still hot.

The animal rose onto four thin legs that ended in huge white paws and looked straight at her. Terry took in the wide pale chest, the cinnamon-colored ruff, the eyes outlined in kohl. It raised its head and slowly wagged its thick brush of tail back and forth.

"Go home, dog," she said.

Probably belonged to a neighbor. Maybe a stray. Just beyond the peeling white fence lay open desert, bisected by a single two-lane highway. Coyotes howled there every night at dusk. She had heard stories of feral dog packs terrorizing residents on rural roads.

"Good dog. Go home."

The animal sat. Cocked its head to the right.

*Wolf.*

The word floated into her mind, startlingly clear as it plunked into place, the sound reverberating like the dry whisper of wind in a desert canyon.

"How can you be a wolf?" The few wolves that survived in New Mexico were reclusive. They prowled the deep wooded canyons to the north.

The animal's ears flattened. Its tail lowered. It ducked its head and stepped forward.

Terry reached for the broom leaning against the house.

"Go away." She grabbed the broom, but the sound of wheels turning off the paved road onto the gravel driveway startled the animal. Like a streak of red smoke, it ran around the house and disappeared.

51

The squared-off two-tone blue pickup stopped by the gate.

"Hi, Karl," Terry called. "I might have a load."

Karl emerged from the cab and touched his Stetson in greeting. He inspected the bags. "Not quite," he decided. "Are you going to keep that old washer in the garage?"

"It doesn't work."

"I could drop it off at the Goodwill. Take the rest to the dump. If you think you're done throwin' out."

"This is the last of it. I took Mom's clothes to the thrift store."

Karl grabbed a bag in each hand and threw them into the truck. "Gonna miss your Ma. Lots of folks will. But after your Dad passed, she sat on that porch just waitin' for the call."

As that image formed in Terry's mind, she cringed. "I asked her to stay with me in San Francisco, but she loved this place. She always said she found her real home in the desert."

Karl finished loading the bags. "If you want to open the garage, I'll just throw that washer in and get out of your hair."

"You've been a big help, these last weeks."

"That's what neighbors do."

"You live ten miles away." There was so much distance between things here that people thought of space differently. At home, neighbors lived in the same building.

She had always lived in cities—first in Minneapolis, later Berkeley for college, then San Francisco. She had never liked this desolate land where her parents had retired and where her mother had lived alone for the last five years.

The billboards proclaimed it the Land of Enchantment, but to her it was the land of sagebrush and sand. Rattlers. Gila monsters. Dinosaur bones. So much open space it made her want to floor the accelerator as she drove through it. Her mother had wanted her to relocate. Every time she visited, Esther told her about the poets and writers who lived in the area.

"Mom, I live in San Francisco," she had said just before Esther got sick. "I work in publishing. I copyedit books. My poems get published. There is no better place for a writer."

The smile her mother gave her made her wish she could take back her exasperated words. But now here she was, living in the little house for the last two months of Esther's illness and another month of getting the house ready to be rented.

She opened the garage door. Karl pulled a hand truck out of his pickup and wrestled the old appliance into the bed.

"You'll be looking for a tenant for the place?" Karl asked after he had climbed back into the cab.

She pushed her Giants cap high on her forehead. "If you hear of anybody, give them my number, okay?"

"Bet you could live here a lot cheaper than you do in the city."

She laughed. "No kidding."

Esther had said the same thing not long before she died. *There are worse places to be, and more here than you can see, darling.* She had looked around her bedroom and nodded as if she were speaking to a room full of people.

"Thanks again, Karl."

"I'll be in touch." The truck kicked up so much gravel leaving, it disappeared into a dust devil.

Terry stood in the dried-up yard as the dust settled around her. She wondered what she would do after she finished with the house. She had lost her job a month before her mother got so sick she needed help. Orlando had decided he needed more space, from her, she assumed, and moved to New York to prove himself as an artist. She hadn't heard from him once. Her roommate had taken over the apartment, but there was no telling how long that would last.

The dark weight in the center of her chest that threatened to overpower her best intentions pushed against her ribs. Here she was in the middle of nowhere. With nothing to do.

She sat on the porch steps and looked at the emptiness. She sat there until the coyotes started howling and the sun went down and the moon rose over the distant mountains, big and yellow and bright enough to fade out the millions of stars she knew were there.

♪♪♪

Terry climbed down the ladder to inspect her handiwork. The sand-colored paint worked in the living room. When she cleaned up the mess and put back the furniture, minus the two ugly recliners tagged to be sold, the room would look pretty good.

*Good enough to live in.*

The voice was so clear, she turned to answer, thinking someone had seen the *For Rent* sign and come to the door. Instead, she faced the cinnamon-colored wolf. It stood in the hallway that led to the bedrooms, ears forward, mouth slightly open, as if it were smiling.

She lifted her right hand and pointed her paintbrush at the animal. "Get out of here," she said loudly.

With her left hand, she fished in her pocket for her phone.

The animal sat and wagged its thick tail against the floor.

"How did you get in here, dog?"

*Wolf.*

"Fine. Wolf. Whatever. What do you want? And why am I talking to you?"

The animal stared into her eyes.

She waved her paintbrush again. "You need to get out of here, boy. Or I'm going to call animal control."

The wolf's ears disappeared into its ruff. It stopped smiling.

*I do not wish to stay here. And, I am female.*

The wolf turned and stalked down the hall.

Terry waited until it disappeared into the smallest bedroom, the one Esther had used for a sewing room. She dropped the paintbrush and picked up a broom. The door to the room was ajar. Very slowly, she used the broom to push open the door. She expected to see that she had left one of the windows open, but both were closed. The room was empty. No sign of the dog. Wolf. She checked the closet. Empty.

She must be losing it. There were no animals in the house. Better have some lunch and finish up the painting.

♫♫♫

Terry hiked into the canyon and followed a rivulet of a stream up from the desert floor through stands of pinon pine and squat juniper, past towering granite boulders and through a sandstone slot until she came to the little waterfall. There was nothing like this at home. She stripped off her shirt and stood under the trickle of water flowing down from the top of Pacheco Peak.

Drying off in the sun, she listened to the desert. Funny how she used to think it was quiet. If you listened, you could hear the plaintive calls of prairie dogs, birds quarreling in the junipers, the tiny sounds lizards made scrambling over indentations in the sand, looking like miniatures of the huge lizards that had roamed this land when it was the shore of a shallow sea. She looked out over the plain below stretching to the horizon. Suddenly it struck her. She was on the bottom of what had once been an ocean.

*Like home.*

She twisted around. The cinnamon wolf sat on the trail near the waterfall. Her heart pounded. "How can you be here?"

The wolf's ears pricked forward. *This is my home.*

Terry picked up a rock and pitched it at the wolf. It missed by a yard. The wolf rose and walked down the trail, tail and head high, deliberately picking her way around the rocks. She passed Terry and continued down toward the desert floor. When she came to a bend that would take her out of sight, she turned and raised her muzzle as if she were going to howl. *Why do you fear what you have always sought?*

Terry picked up another rock and slammed it into the sand. The wolf walked around a large rock and disappeared. She thought of all the poems she had written about the mysteries of deep water, how often she had imagined walking on the bottom of the sea.

"Here it is," she muttered to herself. "Right in front of me. Damn that wolf."

She picked up her pack and started down the trail, hoping to catch up with it, but there was no sign of the wolf, no paw prints on the bank of the stream, and nothing howled in the distance.

♪♪♪

No one wanted to rent the little house. Terry stayed on. She hiked the mountains and the desert and she wrote about life on the bottom of the inland sea. She thought about Orlando and wondered if she had really loved him. She thought about things Esther had said in her last weeks, snatches of conversation that seemed to belie her view of her mother as placid, conventional, and accepting of whatever came her way.

I had to fight your father to leave Minneapolis, but it was worth it.

If you spend all your time in cities, you can miss the sound of your own voice.

Out here, even the air speaks.

At the time, she thought her mother's mind was wandering, but now, as the desert seeped into her, Terry wondered if she had known Esther at all.

On the last day of September, she set out to explore Rockhound State Park, where you could pick up and carry away any minerals you could find.

As she drove down a county road that paralleled Interstate 10, she saw a shadow on her left side. It gained on her until it was opposite the car door. She slowed to glance at it and almost screamed.

The cinnamon wolf was loping along beside the car. Terry pulled onto the shoulder and stopped. She gripped the steering wheel with both hands to stop them from shaking. The wolf stopped ahead of her and sat, head cocked, sides heaving.

"Why are you following me?" she called out the window.

Come with me.

"I have other plans and anyway, you're not real."

As real as you.

Terry rolled up her window and floored the accelerator. When she came to a sign for Deming, she drove into the town and stopped at the first restaurant she found. The faded plastic flowers on the brown laminate tables looked more real than she felt. She glanced out the window. No wolf. A tired waitress brought her tacos and coffee. After she had eaten, she decided that living in the desert was affecting her mind.

In the car, she pulled out her map. She had passed the exit for the state park, but she spotted an area called

"Grandmother Mountain" west of Deming and decided to head for it.

The mountain range rose in the distance, stark and lifeless, with rocks that looked like they had been on guard since the earth's crust had cooled. She left the interstate and turned onto a two-lane county road. She slowed and breathed in the desert. It breathed around her, cradling her in its palm. She had forgotten about the cinnamon wolf until she topped a rise and had to brake hard to avoid running her down. The wolf sat in the middle of the road, squarely on the white center line.

Tires squealing, the Honda swerved. It stopped inches from the wolf's nose.

"What are you doing?" Terry yelled out the window. "I could have killed you."

The wolf raised her head and smiled.

Terry turned off the ignition. Her hands shook. *This is not a mind game. This is a real wolf.*

"What are you doing?" she called.

Turn here.

"There's nowhere to go."

Turn.

In every direction stretched sand and creosote bushes. No sign of civilization. Then, something clicked in her mind and she saw, under the sand, buried so long it had been lost from memory, a road stretching as far as the mountains on the northern horizon. It shone as if it were paved with bronze.

"Where does it go?" she asked the wolf.

Home.

The word entered Terry's mind, and floated down into her body. As the rose-colored word entered the dark place inside her, she began to cry. She cried for Orlando who hadn't loved her, and for her mother who had lived alone for so long, and for all the times she had pulled back when she should have moved forward.

The wolf jumped up to the car, put her paws on the door, and thrust her head through the open window. She pushed her nose against Terry's neck. It was cold and moist. *Follow me.*

Terry found a tissue and blew her nose. "Home, huh?" She scratched the wolf's silky ears and started to say no, I don't want to get lost, but different words came out.

"Okay. Let's go."

The wolf yelped once, a high, happy sound, and loped away.

The miles drifted by as if the day had shifted into slow motion. The sun fell toward the horizon. Everything looked the same. Dusty sage, chamisa, an occasional creosote bush, prickly pear everywhere. The Honda rocked up and down over the packed mud. She stopped thinking about where she was going. She stopped thinking about her mother and about why Orlando had left. There was only the path under her wheels and the wolf.

She didn't see how deep the hole was until her left front wheel sank into thick sand. She wrenched hard on the steering wheel. The right tire lifted part way out, coming to rest on the side of the ditch. She scrambled out to look. The left rear wheel was buried in sand while the right one spun slowly in midair.

"I'm stuck," she yelled to the wolf.

Walk from here.

"Walk where? There's nothing here but too much sun."

Come.

"Come where? Farther into this desert?"

Yes.

"No. I'm going back to the road." She reached for the car door.

A sound froze her in place. A howl. One low, mournful note that escalated slowly, a crescendo that reverberated through her cells. Backing away from the car, she looked around. The cinnamon wolf was not howling. She stood erect, tail pointed straight out, ears forward, mouth slightly open. What was going on? Was there another wolf?

It came from the east, streaking across the sand, a fluid black shape, running with mouth open and tongue sliding over its lips. Terry scrambled down the ditch toward the car, intending to get in and lock the door. Before she could, the black wolf veered toward the cinnamon wolf. She leaped into the air, emitting low whines. The black wolf slowed to a trot, then stopped and sat, ears pricked and tongue lolling.

The cinnamon wolf approached the black wolf with her head and tail down. She crawled the last few steps so her head was under his neck. She gently bit his jaw; he reached down to nuzzle her.

They tore off. The black caught and pinned the cinnamon. She squirmed away, jumped up, and ran off, with him in pursuit. He stopped. She raced at him and leaped. They kept up what was clearly a game of tag for more than five minutes.

Abruptly, they flopped down on the sand a few yards from her car and lay sprawled against each other.

An unbidden thought dropped into her mind. *This is why I'm here.* She laughed out loud.

The cinnamon wolf grinned at her over the black wolf's shoulder. *This is my mate.*

Terry climbed out of the ditch. "Does he speak?"

Not as I do. Come. We will show you the way.

She watched them start off, in the same direction as before, with quick, backward glances at her. Her fear had evaporated. She picked up her water bottle. It was rough going but she was wearing boots and the wolves moved slowly. She fell into a rhythm, slow and steady over the sand. As their shadows grew longer, they picked up their pace.

She tried to move faster, but soon the wolves were out of sight. She stopped.

The howls began. The female started, she was sure, a high clear note. A lower tone from the male. The notes grew, higher and deeper until the sound filled the desert. She followed the sound and came upon them sitting side by side, heads raised, open mouths pointing toward the sky.

The wolves stopped howling and trotted to her, thrusting their noses into her hands and whining softly. She sat on the sand and stroked their thick fur. They licked her face.

Over their heads, she saw a flame in the distance. She thought a juniper tree must have caught fire, spontaneous combustion after the heat of the day. The flame grew larger.

"Look," she said to the wolves. "Something is on fire."

The cinnamon wolf whined.

The flame coming toward them was no bush on fire, but something foreign and frightening, yards across at its base, tapering as it rose twenty feet or more. Her body wanted to run from this thing, but she was frozen. "What is it?" she whispered.

*She comes to speak to you.* The wolf poked her hand with a cold nose.

The flame stopped a hundred yards away. She stood, flanked by the wolves. The flame burned more red than orange. It assumed a vaguely human shape with what could be a face, long, wild hair, and beckoning arms. Terry's body quivered as she realized this flame was a living being.

"I'm here," she heard herself say.

The flame moved closer. One fiery hand extended. Terry stepped forward. She took another step, feeling a tug in her chest as if she were being pulled by an invisible cord. She went slowly, feeling the crunch of sand under her boots, knowing this was why the wolf had come for her. She lifted her arms to the arms of flame. Just before they met, she wondered why her skin did not feel hot.

A voice boomed in her ears. She tried to turn, but moving was meaningless. The flames were everywhere. A sphere coalesced in their center, like a window forming. It swirled indigo and wine-red. It contained all the colors, but they mixed and merged as if they were dancing, showing first one face, then another. The sphere assumed a more defined shape. The colors blazed and merged into a golden purple. The sphere pulsed in a slow rhythm like the beating of a beloved heart.

One by one, individual colors rose from the purple and dropped into the flame. A string of bright red fell. A triangle of forest green. A circle of blue. Shapes of every color dropped into the flames. As the shapes dropped away, the image blurred, the colors fading until only a golden circle remained.

Terry looked down and saw herself standing in the flames, wearing her jeans and a wrinkled white shirt. She wiggled her toes inside her hiking boots. Still solid. Her mind whirled so fast, it lost track of where it was going and fell silent. She smiled.

The golden circle faded. By the time she noticed the flames dissolving, they were gone.The mountains blazed red from the setting sun. She expected to see the wolves trot out from behind a rock, but there was no movement and no sound except for the call of a raven.

She turned in a circle. A small, cloaked figure sat on a flat rock not thirty feet away. A black garment dragged the ground; a shawl covered all but the eyes. A wrinkled hand emerged from the blackness, turquoise and silver rings on every finger. It clutched a stick leaning against the rock. The figure pulled herself up with the stick and faced Terry.

What Terry could see of her face—thin lips, sharp nose, deep-set eyes—was so deeply lined that Terry was shocked at how old she must be.

"The wolf hunt has gone well, I see." The voice rasped with age and desert air.

"I'm sorry?"

The old woman waved her other hand in the air. "You survived the flame."

Terry wanted to ask who she was but did not dare. "I'm looking for my wolf."

"She has joined the pack for the hunt. She will return tomorrow if you call."

"I see." Terry's knees trembled. She decided to sit down on the nearest rock.

"You survived the flame," the old woman repeated. "Not all who meet her do."

"What happens to them?"

The old woman shrugged.

"I don't know what's going on."

The crone opened her eyes wide. Terry saw two pools of utter blackness. The pools turned into a midnight sky. She blinked back tears. When she looked again, the crone's eyes were wrinkled slits.

The crone nodded. "It's not easy to make friends with a wolf, but you have done that. It's not easy to walk out of a desert, but you can do that too."

"I'm not so sure."

"You have believed what you have been told. There is more to know. Others of your line have done it."

"I have no line. No parents. No children."

"Women live alone on the edge of a desert for a reason," the crone said. "It is not a lonely place for those who have survived the flame." She lowered her hand into the folds of her dress.

"What do you know of me?"

The crone shook her head. "I am only passing by. I saw you enter the flame. What you do now is your business. If you wish to return the way you came, your car is that way." She raised her stick and pointed. She turned and pointed her stick in the other direction, toward the mountains. "I go there. You may come if you wish."

Without waiting for an answer, she hobbled away.

Terry listened. The desert was alive with rustlings, sage moving in the breeze, tiny scurrying feet. In the distance, a wolf howled.

The old woman was melting into the darkness. Terry found herself moving. Even though her legs felt like lead, she put one foot in front of the other. When she caught up with the crone, she fell in behind. Neither spoke. They walked until they came to the base of the first mountain, marked by a small stream and two elderly cottonwood trees. They refreshed themselves with the most delicious water Terry had ever tasted. Without speaking, they lay down under the trees to rest.

At dawn, Terry awoke to find the cinnamon wolf sitting by the stream, looking at her with the familiar open-mouthed grin. She sat up and grinned back. She rose and shook sand from her clothing.

The wolf trotted over and thrust her nose into Terry's hand.

Where was the old woman?

Up there.

Terry looked. A hundred feet up a steep trail, the crone stood, leaning on her stick. One gnarled hand rose in greeting.

The dark weight in Terry's chest was gone.

"Time to go," she said to the cinnamon wolf.

They drank from the stream. Terry filled her water bottle. Together they walked up the narrow trail that led to the top of the mountain as the sun rose, casting the desert rocks and the sand and the juniper trees in a soft golden light that seemed to go on forever.

# THEY FOLLOWED ME

The angel came out of the sea at two hours past midnight, three nights after the moon was full. Not what I would have expected.

I drove across the whole damned country in winter to get away from the ones who followed me. On the route that wound through the south since I'd never seen that part of the country and then north in California. I ran out of steam in a tiny town on the Oregon coast and checked into the Heron Motel on Sand Dunes Road. For most of two days, I slept, thinking I was finally safe.

But when I walked out of that motel on the third day, feeling pretty good about myself, there they were, huddled in a tight group, backed up against the towering sand dunes. They all faced the same direction, silent and still like a bunch of robots waiting for someone to switch on their power.

I didn't look at them directly, just glanced sideways, figuring the less attention they received the better. I walked around them to the beach. During the trip from

Maine, they had picked up some recruits; there must have been a hundred of them.

In the beginning, they had hummed. In harmony. I was living in Arizona than, and one day when I was walking in the desert, they appeared over a rise studded with organ pipe cactus. They stood staring at me as I studied a petroglyph of a labyrinth that had been chipped out of the rock a thousand years ago. There were only six or seven of them then. I thought they were a hiking group and made the mistake of waving. That's when the humming started.

After that, I saw them every time I walked in the desert. They would appear out of nowhere, my strange entourage that looked too real to be a hallucination, but what else could it be? I had never been prey to flights of fancy, but, then, how do you ever know? Maybe my vaunted rationality was slipping. The humming group was hard to fit into my worldview.

I theorized that they were desert survivalists but then I happened upon some real survivalists one Sunday afternoon, complete with fatigues, rifles and complicated hand signals. They made my group look like a Sunday school choir. I got out of there as fast as I could. If I were going to be haunted, singing was better than shooting.

The group kept growing and the humming got more complicated, never any tune I recognized. Part of me

71

knew this was not as much of a mystery as it seemed, but that part scared the hell out of the rest of me. I decided to quit my job and move back to the Maine coast, on the theory that the ones who followed me needed sand and creosote bushes, as if they were a kind of mobile cactus.

While I found a place to rent and looked for work, I was free of them. For maybe two weeks. I settled into a tiny house on a hill overlooking the coast near where I had grown up and told myself I had handled the situation as well as could be expected. Then they materialized on the beach one morning, a raggedy chorus in winter coats and mufflers. I knew I was in trouble.

I did my best to ignore them. Took a job writing code for an educational publisher in Bangor, commuting two days a week and working at home the rest of the time. I stayed busy and off the beach. Didn't even glance out the window. Didn't see them for a month. I was sure I had licked it, whatever it was.

Then they migrated into my front yard. They grouped themselves under a big maple tree that looked like it belonged on a brochure for a leaf tour of New England, except it was spring by then, so everything was green. The first time I saw them there, my body seized up. I stood at that window like a frozen statue, wondering if I had died and just hadn't noticed.

For the first time, I understood the attraction of guns. For an awful moment, I imagined myself walking into the yard and mowing them down in a hail of bullets. But I don't believe in violence, especially with hallucinations, so I went out and told them to lay off the fucking humming.

The group had grown to about thirty individuals. To my amazement, they listened. The humming stopped. They went completely silent and never made another peep. After that, I calmed down and went through a phase of trying to reason with them. Have a chat. Convince them they would be better off under someone else's tree.

I tried to figure out who was the leader, but they didn't seem to have one. Every day, different people stood at the front of the group. They seemed to listen when I spoke, but they never nodded or smiled or did any of the things living people do when they're addressed. I decided they were ghosts.

The part of me that knew what was going on smiled a little at that and tried to give the rest of me some friendly advice, but I shut it down and went for a run. I was an educational programmer. I built games so kids could learn to read. Ghosts, I didn't want to know about.

I bought heavy drapes for the front window and never opened them. I left the house by the back door, got into my car, and backed out, never looking toward the tree. None of this helped. The ghosts ruled my life.

The one time I invited a woman to the house, she kept looking out the window and asking about the shadows moving under my tree. I got that I was not the only one who could see them. I became a recluse.

The group kept growing. There was quite a variety among the ghost people, as I now thought of them. They were all ages, all colors, young, old, even a couple of kids. No one I had ever seen before. I considered that they wanted me to join them. I had given up the idea that I was already dead, but maybe it was my time, and they were some kind of silent welcoming committee.

When I gathered my courage to ask them about it, they all took two steps backward, in unison, and huddled closer together. The ones in the front looked so nervous, I never mentioned it again. By the following winter, I was out of ideas and decided to run as far and as fast as I could. Hence Oregon.

When the ghost people followed me down to the empty beach, trudged over the sand dunes, and formed themselves into a long straight line, I knew the only options left were to catch a boat to Japan or drown my sorrows in the gray winter sea. That required some contemplation, so I holed up at the Heron Motel while I tried to imagine what it would be like to be dead.

I hadn't quite made up my mind when the angel walked out of the sea.

I couldn't sleep that night and went down to the beach around midnight, bundled in a down coat, wool hat, muffler, mittens, and boots. At the water's edge, I made a fire with driftwood and sat watching the breakers crash against the shore. Breaking waves soothe me, so I was actually enjoying myself when I noticed a huge, pale gray figure skimming over the water, way past the breakers. I thought it was another ghost coming to join my pack. But this thing was so big, it was clearly nothing human, either alive or dead.

Fifty feet tall, at least. As it came closer, it seemed to shrink, and by the time it reached the shore, it was only two or three heads taller than me. It waded through the breakers like anyone might. When it reached the hard sand, I saw that, in addition to its long gray robe, it wore high boots of the same gray material. The boots had wings on each side.

On the wet sand it stopped and pulled off its boots. Held them in one hand. Motioned with the other to my fire.

"May I join you?" it asked me in a perfectly normal voice. It was towering over me at this point. I motioned for it to sit down. I was fascinated by the wings on the boots and watched as it carefully placed them near the fire.

"They get heavy when they're wet," it said. "I saw your fire, and thought I could dry them out."

"Be my guest." Then I remembered where I had seen winged boots before. A book on mythology. I blurted out, "Are you Hermes?"

The angel laughed so hard it lost its clear definition. I felt a solid hand on my shoulder. "Sorry," it said. "I'm not laughing at you. It's a common misconception that only Hermes wears winged sandals. We all wear them. And they're not even sandals."

Solid again, the angel turned and looked straight at me. I could see its robe clearly, shimmering folds of some material clearly not native to Earth. It appeared to be a malleable semi-liquid. Its face was vague. Very large. Human shaped, with deep dark eyes and a kind mouth, but glowing with an internal light that made it hard to pin down the exact features.

"I didn't mean to offend," I said.

"None taken, I've been meaning to visit you. I see you've done a wonderful job." It motioned with its incredibly long arm to the line of ghost-people. They had grown excited when the angel came ashore and now were bouncing on their feet, swaying from side to side. The humming had started again.

"With what?" I was honestly confused.

The angel smiled, and the whole beach seemed to light up. "It's difficult down here, isn't it?" it said in a compassionate voice. "Forgetting who you are must be disconcerting. We are aware of the sacrifices you humans make. We appreciate your efforts."

I must have look as confused as I felt, because the angel gestured again to the line of ghosts. "You are a gatherer," it said. "You decided to spend your time here finding what was lost. You've made a wonderful start with these souls. Look how many you've found."

I turned around to look at the line. It had grown again. "I don't know anything about that," I said.

"Of course not," said the angel. "But you did it anyway. I salute you. Perhaps now you would like a respite from your duty. A vacation, as it were. Time to find a partner. Perhaps start a family."

"Is this some kind of joke? These people are all dead. Am I dying too?"

The angel smiled. "You are quite alive. I see this has been stressful for you. Gathering is not an easy occupation. I will take these you have found and escort them to their next destination. If you wish to resume your gathering, you can do so when you're ready. Again, your efforts are much appreciated. Your record will be noted. Now I will leave you to resume your life. Ah, I see that my boots are dry."

The angel slipped the gray boots back on its feet. I didn't realize until afterward that I didn't actually see its feet, but I attributed that to the glow emanating from its body. At any rate, it got its boots back on, stood up, and raised one arm high above its head.

I watched as the line of ghosts came forward, slowly forming themselves into another line behind the angel.

They did not hurry or push or have any disagreements about order. They knew exactly what to do.

The angel walked into the water. Behind it came the line of my followers. As each one passed, they smiled and nodded. Some put their hands together in front of their hearts.

The angel walked out through the breakers. All the ghost-people followed. The light from the moon shone on the dark water. It looked like they were walking into a long silver tunnel. Just before they disappeared, they turned and waved. I waved back. Then they were gone.

I stayed on the beach until the first light appeared over the eastern mountains. There was no fog and it looked like the day would be clear and cold. I looked around, half expecting to see the ones who had followed me, but they were really gone. I felt good. Alone. Ready for whatever would come next. I decided to go back to the Heron Motel for a few hours' sleep before I started home.

When I opened the door to my room, a tiny woman— jet black curls, ivory skin, pink rosebud mouth—all decked out in red and gold, was sitting on the bed, her shapely legs crossed demurely under a shimmering transparent skirt.

"How did you get in here?" I asked.

"The window was unlocked," she answered, and jumped to the floor. She walked toward me. The top of her head came to just above my knee.

"I heard you're traveling back to the Maine woods. I'm a wood nymph. Got stranded here a few years back. Can't handle the fog. Thought I might catch a ride home."

I sat on the chair by the window so I could look into her face. The rosebud bloomed. I was transfixed at how beautiful she was. "How did you know that?"

"Word gets around."

"Well," I said. "I wouldn't mind some company. It's a long ride."

She gave me a smile that even I could not mistake and placed her tiny white hand in mine. The trip back was shaping up to be pretty interesting.

She tugged on my hand, so I rose and walked across the room to the bed. I sat down and lifted her up by the waist so she could sit beside me.

"Thank you," she said prettily, and leaned against my arm. She was soft and very warm.

"And by the way, I have a few friends. If you don't mind."

∞

# INSEMINATION

Dorothy knew her way around the dream world. She had been a ghost-messenger so long she hardly ever misjudged her coordinates and she was adept at dream design, her specialty in the Afterlife Evolution Program.

As Dorothy peered through the familiar time tunnel into her sister's bedroom, she noticed that Eva was asleep, alone again in her large comfortable bed. Eva's brow creased as she tossed her head on the pillow.

Bringing her attention back to the dream world, Dorothy glanced around her creation, a reasonable facsimile of the garden in their childhood home, summer flowers everywhere, the rows of peonies particularly evocative. She smiled as she arranged her luminescent form on the wooden swing. Her supervisor would be pleased.

She didn't wait long for her sister to appear. Eva's eyelids fluttered as she relaxed into deep sleep. While Dorothy was still appreciating the bouquet of the ivory peony blossoms, Eva appeared on the swing beside her.

"Eva. It's me. Dorothy."

Eva's eyes widened. "You surprised me."

"How are you, Sis?"

"Oh, Dorothy, I'm so glad to see you. And look where we are. I loved playing in this garden when we were children. We were happy then, weren't we? Do you remember?"

"Of course I remember. That's why I brought you here."

Eva looked down at her bare feet resting in thick grass. "Those were such happy times. Everything's different now. I didn't think my life was going to turn out like this."

"Like what?"

"I don't have anyone to talk to. Not really. Not like we used to talk together. All night sometimes."

"You can talk to me now."

Eva moved closer to her sister and lowered her voice. "It's Peter. He works late most nights, and when he is home, all he does is watch TV. We hardly ever go out. Sometimes I feel like screaming. You don't know how much I've missed you since you died."

She tried to lean against her older sister, but the ghost had risen from the wooden swing suspended from two branches of an elderly magnolia tree. Eva, unable to check her forward momentum, landed face down on the wooden slats.

"Of course I do," Dorothy said. She frowned as her sister hastily righted herself, smoothing the skirt of her nightgown with trembling fingers. "Why do you think I came to see you? It's a big universe, you know. Do you think it's easy to arrive at exactly this place at a time when you're asleep?"

"I suppose not. I haven't dreamed of you for ages. I thought you were busy."

"I have been busy, but it takes two to make a dream, and plenty of juggling of space-time probabilities. Math was never my best subject, and ... oh, never mind." She stopped, embarrassed to catch herself complaining. "And stop crying, will you? I don't know how you do that, dream and cry at the same time. No, don't tell me. I haven't got time for nonsense."

Dorothy still felt guilty about leaving Eva on her own all those years ago. These visits were her way of making amends. "I came to see you, Eva, to see how you're getting along. You've been married a long time now."

"Twelve years." Eva dried her eyes with the hem of her nightgown. "I'm thirty-four. You would be thirty-eight if you'd lived."

Dorothy suppressed a smile. She still looked seventeen, a bit pale from the meningitis, but among the ghost-messengers, a pale complexion was a mark of beauty. "So what's the problem? He makes a decent living; you have a beautiful home. What's stopping you from having a child?"

Eva blushed. "It may not be in the stars."

"What have the stars got to do with it? Do you know how far away the stars are? If you want to know what's affecting your life, you might try paying more attention to the spirit world."

"The what?"

"The spirit world, Eva. My world." Dorothy looked at Eva's stricken face. "Uh, sorry, Sis."

"I really thought it was the stars."

Dorothy forced herself to think about the child who would transform her sister's life. She decided to try again.

"Your daughter wants you to honor her contract, Eva. She's been waiting a long time to be born. She's very picky about the space-time intersections; they have to be exactly right for her to accomplish her goals. The time is now. You've agreed to be her mother. That's what I came to tell you. It's time. Past time actually."

"I didn't sign any contract. What are you talking about?" She giggled. "You made that up, didn't you?"

The ghost rolled her eyes. "I don't make things up, and you did sign something. Not on paper. It's a spiritual agreement. Do you remember how you always said you wanted children?"

Eva turned away. Her fingers twisted in the folds of her nightgown.

"Eva?"

"Yes. Yes, I've said it."

"And haven't you been to every doctor in town trying to figure out why you haven't conceived?"

"Well, yes. I wanted to know why. Peter's family is getting impatient, so I thought I should check. It's strange to be married so long and be...."

"Barren?"

"Don't say that," Eva cried. "I am not barren. I can have a child; all the doctors said so. And there's nothing wrong with Peter either. We're just unlucky."

Dorothy's alignment began to slip.

"Wait," Eva whispered as the ghost faded to a transparent outline. "Don't leave me. Please don't go. I love you so much." She twisted around on the swing, trying to wrap her arms around a dissipating light.

"I can't stay if you lie to me."

"I won't lie. Come back. I'll tell you the truth."

"All right." The ghost made a mental adjustment to her calibration in time, and, suddenly solid again, plunked down on the wooden swing. "We were talking about the contract."

"I don't remember signing anything."

"What about all your prattling about being a mother? Did you think that was idle conversation you could dismiss whenever you felt like it?"

"Yes! Of course I did."

"It didn't occur to you that you might be conveying your intention to the universe."

"What?"

"Or that you might be making an agreement with someone who wants to be born."

"Of course not. How could I? We don't believe in things like that." Tears dripped down her chin.

Eva had a point. Only in her dreams could her sister perceive anything beyond the tip of her own nose. Their whole family had been like that, with more rules about so-called reality than anybody could remember, much less follow. Of course Eva didn't remember her agreement with a soul waiting to be born. And not just any soul either. Out of the ranks of the beings waiting for earthly bodies, somehow her sister had attracted the attention of an Old One.

It seemed an odd choice, but if this Old One believed she could prepare for her teaching mission by growing up in a dysfunctional family, she couldn't ask for a better parent than Eva. And the child would transform Eva's life.

Dorothy had been permitted to peek into her sister's future before she accepted this assignment. Eva would love her daughter fiercely until the day she died. Even Peter would melt when his baby daughter smiled.

Dorothy gazed fondly at her sister who was weeping into her hands. Eva looked older than her years, but it could be the old-fashioned nightgown with its high neck and long sleeves. She thought about suggesting an update in her sister's sleep attire. It might make things run a bit more smoothly with Peter but before she could form the words, she felt a tug in her mind.

Dorothy turned and looked up. A golden door swung open. It revealed a flowing mass of pink and blue light. Sounds emanated from the light, a flat, high pitched whine first, then the Old One's voice fell like raindrops spattering against her forehead. *Tell her it must be soon.*

"Sis." Dorothy put her arm around Eva's shoulder. "I came to tell you about the baby."

"I know." Eva had stopped crying. She was staring at a spot behind Dorothy's shoulder. "I saw her. She's so beautiful. She reached for me. Oh, Dorothy, she loves me already. I was worried I might have a child who didn't love me."

Dorothy glanced over her shoulder. The light had vanished.

"What did you see?"

"The baby, of course. A little girl, all dressed up in a beautiful pink dress with white lace and blue ribbons. She is my daughter. I'm sure of it. I really do have a daughter. The only problem is..."

"What?"

"Peter. Sometimes I think about leaving him. I wonder if it's too late for me to find someone who loves me as much as he loves his job."

"Peter was always obsessed with his business. You knew that from the beginning."

"I know," Eva wailed. "But I wanted to get married."

"We all have problems, Sis. And you want this child, even if your marriage isn't perfect. Peter wants a child too."

"I'm afraid he won't care about a girl."

"It will be fine. I promise."

Eva sniffed. "I do love him, you know."

"I know."

"You do? How?"

"I know a lot of things."

The sisters sat in silence.

"It's better being dead, isn't it?"

"I am happier," Dorothy said. "I will always be beautiful. And I love my job. I call on people and spend time with them. They tell me about their deepest desires, because after all, I'm only a ghost in a dream. Then I whisper something in their ear, and what I whisper is what they remember when they wake up."

"What will you whisper to me?"

The ghost leaned closer. Eva bent her head. Dorothy's lips grazed her hair.

"Keep your agreement. Bear the child."

∫∫∫

From the time tunnel, Dorothy peered at her sister as Dorothy awakened from her dream. Moonlight flooded the bedroom. A wind had risen, and the branches of the willow tree outside the window moaned as they whipped against the windowpane.

Dorothy knew that Eva did not have the focus to remember their meeting, but all that mattered was whether she had caught Dorothy's last words.

Eva opened her eyes. She reached out and patted the other side of the bed, but her hand encountered only cool, smooth sheets. She glanced to her left. She was alone. "I'm almost too old," she said into the pillow.

Downstairs, a door slammed. Another door opened and closed. She jumped out of bed, stepped out of her nightgown, and kicked it into the closet. Before he reached the top of the stairs, she was back under the covers.

When the bedroom door creaked open, her eyes were closed. She sighed deep in her throat and turned over, slowly and luxuriously, so she was in exactly the right position to be awakened when he slipped into bed beside her.

As the connection between them faded, Dorothy smiled. The Old One would be pleased.

∞

# LA LOBA

The crone raised her head as the wind swept down the mountain. It swirled the pale dust into columns that traversed the desert floor like dancing Kachinas and spread a layer of silt over rocks deposited there when the great ice sheets retreated from the land. Within the wind was the call of a lost child. The crone sat in the entrance to her cave, watching and waiting. Later, the wind gentled and whispered in her native language.

She answered. *Now?*

*It is time. You must hurry.*

She gathered her voluminous skirt and rose on spindly legs. The fire had gone out. She would have liked a cup of tea before venturing into the desert heat, but the wind was never wrong. She picked up the cottonwood walking stick she had carved by the banks of the Rio Grande years before and started south, toward the place where the tourists gathered.

∫∫∫

Mia looked up from stirring the canned stew heating on the camp stove. The sudden wind had whipped the lake into motion, creating waves that broke against the beach. Farther out, pelicans had landed for the evening, ruffling their feathers as they rode the waves and emitting chirping sounds that sounded like a raucous orchestra tuning up for a performance.

Allie was wading into the waves, already in water higher than her waist, her golden hair blowing, unmistakable in her pink swimsuit.

"Allie!" Mia started to run.

He was kneeling on the beach, sorting his fishing tackle. At her cry, he looked up. With a few strides, he reached Allie and scooped her into his long arms. Mia noticed how Allie squirmed, how he held her a little longer than necessary, how her daughter broke and ran when he released her.

Allie's skinny arms enclosed her waist. Mia clutched her shoulders. "I told you not to go in the water without me."

Allie gave her the smile that always made Mia feel like she had done at least one worthwhile thing. "I saw a wolf. Then pelicans."

"There are no wolves here, honey. Sit down and eat."

Mia looked across the water to the tufa formation, shaped like a woman with a basket at her side. The ranger had told her its name, Stone Mother, and the legend that her tears had formed Pyramid Lake. When Mia asked why she cried that much, the ranger had smiled and shrugged. "A creation story," he said. "Her husband sent away her children because they fought too much." He shrugged again. "She missed them."

Mia's husband came up carrying his fishing pole and put his heavy arm around Mia's shoulders. She tried not to shiver.

♫♫♫

The west wind blew down from the granite mountains so lovingly sculpted by the retreating ice that they had never changed their shapes nor grown grass upon their gentler slopes. It whistled through the tent flaps, rattling the poles pounded into the hard desert sand and keeping the child awake.

"I hear voices," she whispered from the folds of her bag. Mia reached out of her own bag and caressed Allie's hair. "It's all right, baby. It's just the wind."

"Shut her up," he said, his voice rough with beer.

"Hush, love. Your father's trying to sleep."

Allie pressed her face against Mia's arm.

The wind blew until the deepest part of the night and then stopped as if a faucet left on by mistake switched off.

Mia lifted her head and looked out the window of the tent. A cloud passed over the moon.

She dropped into a dream of heat and rocks ejected from the core of the planet in a wild stream of orange liquid, still too hot to touch. Later, she woke to the call of a wolf howling in the distance. The sound drowned out his snores. She reached for her daughter, but Allie was gone.

∫∫∫

The ranger called the police. They came quickly at the news that a nine year old was missing. Their jeeps and black and white cars tore up the sand and created a cloud of dust. They wore uniforms and guns and searched the campground and the lakeside with their hands hovering over their weapons. They ordered everyone out of the lake.

Mia cried and screamed. She ran up and down in the shallow water, shouting her daughter's name. He tried to hold her, but she fought him with her nails and teeth so he had to let her go.

The police fanned out. They asked for something her daughter had worn. She rummaged in the tent and handed them a shirt, soiled from the previous day when they had eaten ice cream cones in the village. Two black dogs with the long noses of wolves sniffed the shirt, whined, and dragged their handlers away, muzzles pressed to the sand.

"The dogs will find her," he said. He tried to put his arm around her, but she pulled away and would not meet his eyes. "She wandered away," he said. "She's not in the lake."

She bared her teeth. He meant to comfort her, but it no longer mattered what anyone thought. "How do you know? How could you? When have you ever cared what happened to her?"

"That's not fair. She's my daughter too."

"You didn't want her. You didn't want me once she was inside me. She knew it. She always knew it."

A ranger pulled him away. Whispered something in his ear. Patted his shoulder. Mia ran along the shore screaming for Allie.

When the sun was high, they brought in boats and men in rubber suits. They carried long poles and nets and floated up and down the lake, trolling for Mia's daughter. Mia sat on a flat rock and stared into the lake. He tried to coax her down. She ignored him. He brought food, but she would not eat. When the boats floated away to another part of the lake, Mia lay flat on her stomach on the warm rock so she could see into the depths more clearly.

She had been there for hours when an old woman, swathed in black cloth, hobbled up and stood beside her.

After a time, the crone said, "You're not wrong." The woman was so old her face looked like an unbroken mass of creases, her eyes barely slits. She grasped her stick in a hand shaped like a claw.

"What do you mean?"

The crone walked forward until the water sloshed at her knees. With a gnarled finger, she pointed at the water. "She went home."

Mia leaned over the rock and looked where the crone pointed. She thought she had seen something in the cold clear deep. Now she stared more intently.

"Soften your eyes," the crone said. "Look beyond the water."

Mia tried to obey. She saw only ripples spreading from the passage of the rubber boats. She lifted her head to look for her husband. He had gone farther down the beach with the rangers. As they called to each other, their voices sounded like a recording played too fast.

Mia went back to staring into the water. She blinked to clear her vision. When she opened her eyes, structures shimmered on the bottom of the lake. Delicate buildings like a family of tiny elves might inhabit, with elaborate scrollwork on their facades and windows that shone like prisms.

White and pale pink, the buildings undulated with the currents. She saw people, the right size for the buildings, walking on the streets. They joined together in groups. They chatted and laughed. They were dressed in pastels, swirling skirts that moved with the current, capes and elaborate shirts. Some wore hats while others let their long hair flow. Their skin ranged from nearly black to translucent white although most were shades of brown. They all looked happy.

Mia tried to touch one of the buildings. Her hand sloshed through water. She glanced at the crone. "What is it?"

The crone stamped her stick. "Another world." Her mouth worked almost into a smile. "You see?"

"Is Allie there?"

The crone reached for her bare arm. Where the leathery fingers touched, Mia's skin burned. "Your daughter has gone home. You are blessed to see it."

Mia screamed. She threw herself into the water, trying to swim down, trying to reach the tiny people, the structures. She was a strong swimmer but she saw only the sandy bottom and a few stray cottonwood branches.

She surfaced, gasping, and screamed again. The crone had vanished. He was wading toward her, pulling at her, using words she didn't understand. He grabbed her waist, lifted her, and carried her to the shore.

"No," she begged. "She's there. Under the water. Get her. Find her. She's under the water. I saw people. Allie is alive. Help me, please!"

He carried her to the tent. The sun shone white in a pure blue sky. Inside the tent the heat enveloped her. He forced her down on the sleeping bag. She struggled, but he flipped her onto her stomach and pushed her face into the nylon. Someone else came in.

"Help me," she begged. The nylon burned her forehead. Something stabbed her arm. Everything went black.

∫∫∫

"You don't have to go." He stood in the doorway of their bedroom, watching as she placed her clothes into the battered suitcase.

She wondered why he was still there. The marriage had ended the day Allie disappeared. She went to the closet and pulled her two dresses from their hangers, folded them and placed them on top of the jeans.

"I'm done." She pushed down the top of the suitcase and fastened the lock.

He shifted from one foot to the other and propped his other arm against the doorjamb. "I shouldn't have taken you to the hospital. I know that now. But you were hysterical."

"I lost my daughter."

"It was only for three days."

"I might have found her."

"Mia, Allie is not at the bottom of the lake. They dragged it. Something else happened. They're still looking. You know that."

"How do I know?" She yanked the suitcase off the bed. "Because you told me? Why should I believe you?"

He released his arm and shifted again. His shoulders filled the doorway. "You can talk to the sheriff. To the rangers. It's been in the paper. They're still looking."

She picked up the suitcase. "Get out of my way."

As his face reddened, she saw the old anger rise. He wanted to stop her, to throw her against the wall so she couldn't cause him any more trouble, but all that was over now. She challenged him with her eyes. He stepped back.

"Where are you going?"

"To find Allie." She walked out of the room, the weight of the suitcase pulling her to the right, and did not touch him when she passed.

She lifted the suitcase into the hatchback of her old Datsun and clicked the door shut. She backed out of the driveway in the early morning heat of the desert where they had lived during their entire marriage.

*I'm coming, Allie* she thought as she headed toward the road that would take her back to Pyramid Lake.

∫∫∫

The black and white pelicans circled for a landing, graceful predators that folded their huge wings at the last moment as they settled on the dark blue water. Mia had pitched her tent at the water's edge and spent the day sitting on a plastic chair.

After the pelicans arrived, she waded into the lake, gently so she wouldn't disturb them. She looked for the underwater city, but saw only sand and stones. She swam close to the pelicans, staying under the surface, allowing only her face to catch the rays of the dying sun. She got close enough to see the droplets of water clinging to their feathers and the curious gaze in their black eyes.

*Have you seen my daughter*, she thought to them. The largest one turned as if it had heard, and ducked his head under his wing. Mia looked down. The water was clear as ice.

Mia swam back to shore. In knee-deep water, she spied a long curving white bone in the sand and bent to pick it up. She carried it to her plastic chair and placed it on the dry sand. It looked like an animal's rib. Before she packed up for the night, she wrapped the bone in a red handkerchief and put it in her backpack. The next day she found another bone, this one smaller and straighter. Walking along the water's edge, she found a bone that looked like a metatarsal.

On the third day, she started walking. She packed her water bottles, extra socks and a jacket in her pack on top of the bones and headed north. She passed other campers, people fishing, children swimming. After an hour, they thinned out. After two hours, only sea birds and lizards kept her company. She found two more bones.

She slept on the shore. The air blew warm and the sound of the waves lulled her to sleep. She awoke filled with a sense of purpose and continued her northward trek. Three more bones went into her bag. She saw boats in the middle of the lake. Once a ranger waved to her from a distance.

She had passed the tufa structure on the far shore that gave the lake its name when a stooped figure approached. The crone hobbled up to Mia, her cottonwood staff making sucking sounds in the wet sand.

Mia stopped. "I remember you."

The crone regarded her. "They called off the search."

The tears that had seldom stopped ran down Mia's face. "The sheriff is sure she isn't in the lake. They're still searching the desert."

"But you know."

"I do."

The crone nodded. "Are you ready?"

"For what?"

"To find what is lost."

"Is that possible?"

"Anything can be found."

"Will I come back?"

The crone shrugged. "You found bones."

"Yes."

The crone nodded as if she had succeeded in the most important task at hand. Mia adjusted her pack on her shoulders.

They left the shore and followed a narrow trail through sand dunes and thick stands of mesquite. When Mia thought they had left the lake behind, the trail turned and led them back to the water and the campsite of the crone, a simple fire pit. Beside it was a knife, a cup, and two curved white bones. They sat and looked at the water.

From her robe, the crone produced a water bottle. "Drink," she said. "We have a long way to go."

"What is your name?" Mia asked.

"Loba." She smiled. She had two teeth, both yellow.

"What do you do with the bones?"

Loba sipped her water. "Sing," she said. "When it's time. Now we go. There are trees ahead where we can spend the night." She gathered her few belongings into a tattered carrying bag made of canvas. They started north again.

Mia trudged behind her. When they reached the end of the lake, her legs felt like lead. Loba guided her toward two spindly cottonwoods. A patch of grass grew under the trees and there Mia sank down while Loba kindled a fire. Loba produced tea from her bag. When it had brewed, she offered Mia a cup.

The tea gave her the strength to open her pack. She ate some raisins and curled up on her blanket. She slept and dreamed of Allie living with the underwater people. Allie laughed and waved to her. When she awoke, Loba had returned with two more bones.

They headed into open desert. Loba knew where the water holes were, but they had only the food they were carrying. That night, Loba trapped a rabbit with a rope snare and two dead cottonwood branches. They made a fire and devoured the sweet tasting flesh.

Mia noticed that her skin had turned brown and her leg muscles were stronger. They continued to find bones. Sometimes they walked in circles so Loba could locate a bone buried in the sand. Some were long and curved, others small as fingers. Loba's bag drooped with the weight of them when they passed the last gravel road and set out toward the distant hills.

They slept in the open, under stars like diamonds. Wolves howled in the distance. Mia shivered at the sound. Every night she dreamed of Allie. Sometimes in her dreams her daughter howled.

♪♪♪

Mia's flesh sizzled and burned. The blisters on her feet broke open and hardened into scars. She kept her eyes on the sand which made it easier to see the bones and retrieve those she thought Loba would want. When she was right, the crone nodded and opened her bag. Mia deposited each bone gently.

When they reached the hills, they came to a stream lined with desert willows. They drank, and Mia ate the last of her nuts and raisins. Loba set another trap so by nightfall they were roasting desert hare over their fire. Mia's skin had turned as dark as the rabbit meat. She wondered if it would dry up and fall off or if it would melt away, leaving her a walking skeleton.

"I'm burnt," she said to Loba who nodded and poured water from the stream over the embers of the fire.

"It is necessary," the crone answered. "Tomorrow we climb." She pointed with her stick at the rocky hill above them.

"Where are we going?"

"Home." Loba smiled her toothless grin.

∫∫∫

Loba's cave was halfway to the top, a narrow tunnel into the mountain with an entrance too low for Mia to enter without stooping. Inside, the rocks were cool. When she

103

removed her boots and socks, thick sand soothed her bruised feet. Fire had blackened one wall and on the other, Loba's belongings rested. A basket with articles of clothing. Another knife. A large pot. Two metal cups. A water bag.

Mia leaned against the wall of the cave and looked out at the rolling desert while Loba arranged the bones on the sand. It took a long time. She had collected the skull last, with a cry of triumph and a quick glance at Mia. The bones assumed the shape of an animal. Curved ribs, straight legs, a spine, toes, and a tail. She smiled as she worked, and crooned under her breath. When all the bones were in place, she leaned back and looked at Mia.

"It's a dog."

"Wolf."

"What will you do with it?"

"Sing. Breathe. Together."

Mia thought of the gossamer people living under the lake. She thought of her beautiful daughter. She looked at the skeleton of the wolf, and at her own ruined flesh. The pieces came together with a jolt of recognition.

"Anything can be found."

The crone nodded. "If you want it."

"I want it."

Loba closed her eyes. She started to sing, a wordless hum that penetrated Mia's lungs and gave her the

104

strength to join the song. They sang over the bones. All the rest of that day and all night they sang. The bones shone silver under the moonlight illuminating the cave. Wind blew into the cave, ruffling Mia's hair with the fierce tears of souls lost in the desert.

As she sang, Mia found a strength flowing up from deep inside her, through her womb into her heart and lungs, sliding over her tongue and filling her mind with images of Allie as a baby. How sweet she had been in her crib, kicking her chubby legs. Allie walking, falling, laughing in delight. The first words she had spoken.

The song moved in circles that became a spiral. On each turn, Allie grew older. When the song could go no higher, it descended the spiral and the images moved in reverse.

By morning, the skeleton had grown coarse hairs on its back and around its tailbone. They sang louder. When fur appeared on the back and ribs, Loba stopped singing. She breathed over the skeleton. She moved her hands in the air in small, rhythmic motions.

Mia blew her own breath over the bones. For the rest of the day they breathed in unison. When the sun flamed the sky, the skeleton had acquired flesh and a coat of fur. By morning, a fully formed animal stretched out on the sand as if asleep, its long muzzle motionless, its flanks unmoving. The wolf's coat was tawny brown, with black markings around its eyes and ears. It had two white paws. It was female.

Mia wanted it to live, to breathe, to whine with pleasure at being alive. She touched its back. It felt warm. Loba nodded at Mia who started again to sing. She sang her pain and grief at the loss of her daughter. She sang her regret that she had stayed with a man who did not love her. She sang her anger and her fear, her loss of innocence, and her love. Her song echoed out of the cave, down the mountain and over the desert all the way to the lake where it penetrated to the sandy bottom.

Tears streamed down Mia's face but she kept singing and singing and singing. Loba watched from behind wrinkled lids and nodded, keeping the beat of the song with her palm against a rock. When the song rose to its highest point, Loba raised her hand for silence. She whispered, "Now."

The wolf eyes opened. A paw moved. The chest rose and fell. The wolf raised her head and looked at Mia with golden eyes.

She touched the soft fur of the wolf's head. The wolf pushed against her hand and whined.

Loba said, "It is done."

The wolf stretched and rose on her long thin legs. Her tail curved over her back. She thrust her wet nose into Mia's neck. Mia put both arms around the wolf and hugged her. The wolf cocked her head to one side. She looked at Mia, then at Loba, her mouth open in a silly wolf smile.

The wolf shook herself once and whined again. Then she bounded out of the cave, down the narrow trail and across the sand. Mia watched her run with all the abandon of a wild creature. She laughed as the tawny wolf streaked across the sand. When the wolf was barely distinguishable from the sand, Mia stood and nodded to Loba.

Loba hauled herself up. "Go in peace." She raised the stick high and brought it down gently on Mia's head.

Mia felt herself shrinking. Her clothes fell off. She dropped to her knees. Her hands and feet turned into paws. Fur erupted from what was left of her skin.

She smelled insects crawling under the sand and heard the faint drip of water far back in the cave. She stretched her new strong muscles and thrust her muzzle into Loba's hand. The crone caressed her jaw.

She remembered this one who stroked her so gently, but there was no time to lose. She whirled and leaped out of the cave onto the trail. In the distance, the tawny wolf loped toward the horizon, almost out of sight.

Mia ran.

∞

# THE GIRL WHO
# COULDN'T FLY

A thousand beating wings darkened the sky, rumbling like an oncoming storm. I looked up from the fire I was building in the great hearth as the mysterious bird-people approached our village.

"Look, Gar," Roon said. He and I were the same age, but we had grown apart since I was chosen Fire Keeper. "Where are they going?"

I had no answer. We stood watching the beautiful strangers we had never seen at such close range soaring above us.

The bird-people resemble us, but we Kotaks are tall and strong, with dark brown skin, straight hair, and dark eyes, while the bird-people were honey-colored, small, and delicate. They flew with their slim legs tucked up to their chests as their copper-colored wings beat the air. The first ones flew so high I could not see their faces, but as more came, some broke off from the group and flew lower. Their faces were narrow and lighter than ours. Their hair was lighter too, and pulled back tight against their small heads. They stared down at us with huge wide eyes as if they were curious.

"Hello!" I waved my fire stick, hoping one of them would speak, but all I heard was a delicate warble. All over the village, Kotaks came out of their houses and stood silently watching the bird-people pass by.

ʃʃʃ

Three days later, as I built the evening fire, my father, Tu, emerged from the forest carrying a bundle wrapped in his shirt.

He shouted to me. "Gar, call your mother. I have found an injured child."

I ran for the *saba*, where the adult women meet each afternoon for the holy rituals. My mother Téle, who is also the Mother of our village, opened the wooden door. Her sharp eyes sought what had disturbed the daily prayers.

When she saw Tu place his bundle near the hearthstone, she strode across the common. "Who has been injured?" she demanded.

"This child is one of the ones that fly." Tu pulled aside his shirt and pointed to her back where tiny, feathered appendages lay useless. "I found her crawling out of the desert. She has wings, but they have not grown."

"Am I to heal an animal so you can have a pet?" Téle asked.

"When I reached her, she spoke. Can we refuse healing to one who speaks?"

Téle met his eyes. "I refuse healing to no one. But this is a dangerous matter. More so if the bird-people can speak. This is the third time they have flown over our village just before the time of planting. None have ever spoken. And now we have one of their children."

"May I put her in the healing *houle*?" Tu asked. I held my breath.

"Yes," Téle said. "Stay with her. I must look inward." She turned back to the *saba*.

The women waiting in the doorway stepped aside. Someone closed the door behind her. Except on special occasions, only grown women are permitted inside.

The flames from the evening fire were sprinkling sparks in the darkness when Téle emerged from the *saba* and entered the healing *houle*. Because she did this, I knew she had seen a way to heal the child. For six nights, Téle went to the healing *houle*. On the seventh night, when the women's *saba* was finished, she came to the hearth

"Tell Tu the child will recover," she said.

I ran to the *houle*, and Tu let me come inside where the bird-girl lay under a woven blanket. She cried out when she saw me. Her bright green eyes fastened on Tu. He stroked her face. I told him what Téle had said.

"I will stay with her until she can walk," he said. "Have you seen any bird-people today?"

"None," I said. "What happened to this child? Can you talk to her?"

He shook his head. "Her language is too different. If her people do not come for her..."

I did not understand how the beautiful bird-people could leave a child behind to die, but I was ready to take on the duties of an adult Kotak, so the childish questions I might have asked a year ago died on my lips.

The weather was warming. The men of the village were planting the *hooma*, while the women prepared the vegetable gardens. Tu was excused from work to care for the injured child, and I spent more time with the men, learning about planting and which prayers to say for a bountiful harvest. Every evening, I lit the village fire.

One night, as I sat by the hearth, a movement quick as a shadow startled me. I turned. The bird-girl stood beside me.

"You are better," I said, ducking my head so she would understand I meant no harm. She didn't answer. I nodded and ducked my head again. She pointed at the large square stone around the fire pit.

"Yes," I said. "Sit." I gestured with my hand.

She sat, hugging her blanket around her thin shoulders. As the firelight shone on her honey-colored skin, I saw her beauty and realized she was more a young woman than a child. My tongue suddenly felt too large for my mouth. Her green eyes followed my every movement. Golden brown hair hung in waves past her shoulders. I wanted to reach out and stroke that golden hair. Instead I said, "My father found you."

She looked at the ground.

"Why did your people leave you? Were you lost?" I spoke slowly, but she shrank from my voice. More questions crowded my mind, but before I could ask them, she fled. The blanket dropped to her waist. The folded wings, small and delicate, rested between her shoulders. They were reddish-brown, like the color of honey left in a bowl overnight. She pulled the blanket over her shoulders and disappeared into the *houle*.

Later Tu came to sit with me at the hearth. "I will ask your mother to take the child into the *saba*," he said. "The women can speak to her with their minds."

"What will happen to her?"

He shrugged. "Her people are gone." He gestured to his chest, showing me that he understood this with his heart.

The next afternoon passed slowly. At day's end, Tu and I sat together, silent with our thoughts, until the women emerged from the *saba*. Téle came last, holding the bird-girl's hand.

"You were successful?" Tu asked.

Téle nodded. "Her name is Dresa. Her people have left our land and will not return. We have offered to keep her as our own."

"Has Dresa agreed?" Tu asked.

Téle nodded. "She can join Pel's household." Pel is my father's sister. She is the best potter in our village, but she was not blessed with children.

"Will you teach her our language?" Tu asked.

Téle nodded. "We will teach her."

When I heard this, I felt happier than I could explain.

ʃʃʃ

Dresa went to the *saba* several times each week. Soon she could converse with us in our language. In time, she became one of us. She wore the simple garments of our women that fastened at her shoulders and hung straight to her knees. Her wings were hidden, and as with many things that go unseen, we forgot they existed.

Pel taught Dresa to fashion cooking and storage bowls from clay and how to decorate them with stylus and dye. She was quick to learn this art and soon, she had improvised new designs. Her drawings had softer edges and rounder shapes than any we had seen. On her bowls, tall trees sheltered birds with fluttering wings, women danced with children, and animals we had never seen flew through the air.

Everyone loved Dresa, which made me happy, but I felt anger when I learned that Roon often left his own work to hang around Pel's house. The next time I saw him leave the fields early, I followed him. He turned to face me.

"What do you want, Fire Keeper?" he asked, taunting me with the name of my sacred duty.

"It is not what I want, but what Dresa wants," I answered.

He laughed. He was taller and heavier, and the outcome of a fight was far from certain. Pel came out of her house. She stared at us without a trace of a smile, and we both went on our way. Neither of us wished to be caught fighting, which is not honorable among adult Kotaks. Still, Roon taunted me every chance he got. I was beginning to feel I had lost her to him when she invited me into the house when Pel was at the gardens. We sat in the large room surrounded by her pots.

"Where did you learn about these things you have drawn?" I asked her. "I have never seen such animals."

Dresa ducked her head as any Kotak would. "I remember what my mother told me when I was little. I could see the pictures her words formed in my head." She touched a finger to her forehead. "Pictures of our home. I draw them so I never forget."

"Is the winged woman your mother?" All her pictures included a flying woman, sometimes in the center of the design, sometimes a tiny figure in a corner.

"No," she said softly. "That is Florin, my twin."

When I saw tears in her eyes, I put my arm around her shoulders. She did not pull away. Her skin was like silk. My skin grew hot and my mouth felt like the open desert beyond the forest. I dared to move a little closer.

"It is common among us," she said, paying no attention to my quivering heart. "It is a special relationship. I lived with my mother and Florin and all our people on the southern continent of your world for many years. It is warmer there, more like our homeland, but the air is too heavy for us. We could not thrive. In council, it was decided to return to our home. My mother, Kirith, is the leader of our people, and she called for a ship to take us back to Salantia.

Twice we flew to the north, to the cold flat land where it is easiest for the ship to land. Both times the conditions were not right. We had to go back. This time, I am certain the ship came. I no longer feel my people, except in my heart."

I patted her shoulder. Her shining eyes were downcast. Her head rested on my shoulder. I barely dared breathe.

"Kirith knew it would be hard for me. I flew before I walked, but then I grew too quickly. My wings would not support me. Florin is only half my size but much stronger in the air. It is the curse of your beautiful world, Gar, that we Romillians cannot grow properly here. Some, like me, grew too tall too fast. Some were born without wings. Many babies died. It is a terrible tragedy, to lose little children."

I stroked her golden hair.

She looked up at me. "I am lucky to have found you."

"Tell me about your twin," I said, because I could think of nothing else to say.

Her face clouded. "We started out together for the north. Florin and I flew side by side. When we approached your village, I was losing strength. I tried to keep up, but soon everyone was ahead of me. We came to the desert beyond your forest. Florin called my name. I tried to follow the sound of her voice, but I fell to ground in the desert place."

My heart pounded as hard as when the wild bull had chased me in the forest.

"They left you."

Her face was still against my chest. "We had to get to the ship. If Kirith could have carried me, she would have, but no one can fly with such a burden."

"They could have waited until you were older."

"Then more children might have been born."

I held her close. "I am sorry for your grief," I said, "but happy that you came to live with us."

"Oh, Gar, I am blessed." She smiled again. "I thought surely I would die, and instead your people welcomed me. I have a wonderful life here. But the more I go to the *saba*, the more I think of Florin and what we would have become. Without her, I cannot be whole."

Her words made my throat tight. "You are more beautiful than any in our village."

I wanted to protect her from every memory that made her sad. I wanted her to look only to me. I didn't understand why she needed her twin so badly. I didn't understand why I couldn't make her happy. I had no more words to offer, so I stroked the gold-flecked hair until Pel came to ask her to fetch the water for the next meal.

With a touch on my shoulder, she was gone, leaving me to my thoughts that circled like the moon in the night sky, returning each month unchanged and mysterious.

∫∫∫

In the fall, the women spent more time in the *saba*. I thought it was my own impatience that made it seem so, for I wanted more time with Dresa, but then I heard Tu talking with another man about how the *saba* had changed.

"Why has it changed?" I asked when his friend left.

He pretended to be startled. "Were you spying on me again?"

"I was repairing the irrigation ditch."

He grinned. "Our Dresa has upset the *saba*, it seems."

"The *saba* is secret," I said, to annoy him.

"Yes, but not how the women feel about it, as you will discover. Pel tells me that, with Dresa in it, the *saba* has gained power. It has also gained length, which has caused some to complain. Not Pel, of course."

"But Dresa is not a Kotak. How could she affect it so?"

"Who has been talking about the *saba*?" Aunt Pel appeared, looking stern. "What business is it of yours?"

"It is not," I said. "Forgive me, Aunt, I have chores." I turned to leave, but Pel laughed and grabbed my arm.

"Come Gar. Let's sit here in the shade." She sank onto the grass under the nearest tree. "It's a new thing for us, to have a woman of another people in our holy circle. It has changed us. I'm not certain where it will lead."

"What makes you uneasy, sister?" Tu asked.

Pel looked over my head as if she saw something in the air. "Since Dresa joined us, the power of our *saba* is great. We travel farther in our minds. We have found people who live in villages like ours in a valley on the far side of the mountain."

Tu asked, "What is the use of this traveling with your minds?"

"It is good to learn." She looked down at the grass.

"Something bothers you," Tu said.

"We have looked into the heavens," Pel whispered. "We have seen above the place where the clouds form."

"Is this new?"

"We have always looked inward and down into the heart of the Great Mother who nourishes us. We have learned much about what is within us and below us, but never have we looked so far above."

"What did you see?" I asked Pel. "What is beyond the clouds? Did you approach the lights?"

Tu jammed his elbow in my ribs, but Pel did not take offense.

"Beyond the clouds, so far there is no way to know the distance, are other lands. People live there, people like us and not like us. With Dresa in our *saba*, we see these lands and these strange people. They make me afraid."

"Have you seen the Romillians, Aunt? Have you seen Dresa's people?"

Pel looked at me with troubled eyes. "No. But I believe Dresa has."

ʃʃʃ

I knew Roon hated me by the look in his eyes when he saw me with Dresa. I was not the only one who noticed.

Fighting over food or livestock or the right to ask another to make a household is not polite behavior, but it happens. Ways have been devised to assist the Mother of the village to decide the outcome of such altercations.

Since the Mother of our village is also the mother who bore me, it was important to be as correct as possible. When Téle discovered my rivalry with Roon over Dresa, she decided that the village would have a night of feasting and dancing, called the *hora*.

During a *hora*, after the feasting, as the stars open their eyes, all the adults gather around the hearth fire. They dance and jump and exhibit their skills in acrobatics in which we Kotaks take great pride. The dancing continues all night. As people become exhausted, they drop out, until only one of the two who are in conflict is left standing. That person then has the right to whatever was at issue. In this case, either Roon or I could then ask Dresa to make a household with him. If she refused, the other could ask her. She was, of course, not required to accept either of us.

Pel explained all this to Dresa.

On the night chosen for the *hora*, I lit the fire as I always did. Everyone gathered for the feast. We spent hours eating and talking and watching the little ones race around playing their games before they fell asleep on their parents' blankets. I ate little, for I was determined to win the contest.

From a distance, I saw Roon watching me. Whenever our eyes met, he scowled fiercely. Dresa stayed close to Pel. I imagined that this custom of ours seemed crude to her, but she said nothing.

When the dancing started, I built up the fire so the flames leaped for the sky. Tu indicated that he would keep the flames for me so I was free to concentrate on my dance.

As the flames grew, the younger men began to dance, jumping and leaping as high as the flames themselves. A group of young women joined in. After a time, all were dancing, young and old. Our moving bodies filled all the empty space around the hearth.

Tu and Téle came to dance beside me in the inner part of the circle and even Dresa joined in, though she had never danced before. We leaped higher and danced longer than anyone had ever done. We danced until the tallest women and the strongest men fell into each other's arms to sleep while the dancing fire whispered all it had seen of that night and the nights gone by and those yet to come.

Tu stayed awake to feed the fire. In the darkest part of the night, only Roon and I still danced. We leapt over the sleeping bodies around the hearth and turned over in the air, landing on our feet and immediately jumping up again to see who could leap the highest.

When the first gray light appeared, I could no longer feel my legs. By then, the dancing fire had gone to embers. Téle, wrapped in her blanket, watched from the hearth along with another elder woman.

Now we danced slowly, moving around the circle with heavy feet. I saw Roon on the other side of the courtyard, readying for a run. I turned my back to find the best place from which to start my own run, even though I was not certain I could leap again.

Roon raced toward me, his face contorted, his arm upraised. He ran as if he intended to jump straight up into the air, as we had both done earlier in the evening. But his foot struck something—a stone, a corner of a blanket— and he stumbled. He flailed his arms trying to save himself, but he fell flat in the dust.

I danced around the circle toward him. He tried to rise, but instead cried out and grasped his left knee with both hands.

Téle went to him. I danced closer so I could hear her words.

"Are you injured?" she asked him.

He made a terrible face and nodded yes.

"Then Gar has won the dance."

I fell on the ground while Tu woke two men to help Roon to his sleeping place so his leg could be tended. Téle pulled me up and walked with me to my sleeping place.

There I slept for most of the day until it was time to light the evening fire again.

∫∫∫

The next afternoon, when I returned from the fields, I went to Pel's house to see Dresa. She met me at the door wearing her best shawl and the turquoise pendant that Pel had made in the shape of a great bird. I thought she was pleased that I had won the contest.

"Dresa," I began, even though my mouth felt like dust.

"Wait, Gar." She touched my arm. "Something wonderful has happened. Even more wonderful than you winning the dance." As she smiled, the light from the window shone on her golden hair. "I want you to come to the *saba* today. You and Tu are invited. It is a special day."

"Téle has agreed?" I asked stupidly.

"She asked me to invite you. Will you come?" She extended her hand.

"Of course." I was breathless at the thought of being in the holy *saba* with her.

She took my hand as we walked through the village toward the *saba*. At the door, Tu waited. When he saw us, he grinned and winked.

Dresa pressed my hand and disappeared through the doorway. Tu shrugged. "I know nothing. But let us enter and see what our women are doing."

Inside was a large round room, dark except for the light of a fire burning in a shallow pit in the center. There was no front or back, so what I had heard was true—in the *saba* all are equal.

Feeling warm bodies all around me and smelling the sweet flesh of the women made me very aware of my maleness. I stuck close to Tu and groped my way to a place on the ground. Murmurs rose from the circle of women, which was four or five deep. The women moved to let us pass. I heard a giggle, then a thump, as Tu took his place.

Finally, I was safe on the ground with Tu on my right. I dared a glance to my left and was relieved to see Aunt Pel. As my eyes adjusted to the dim light, I stole glances around the circle. Dresa sat across from me. Her eyes were closed, but when I looked at her, she opened them and smiled so sweetly my heart unfolded.

Téle started to chant. The women swayed. A hum arose. I concentrated on quieting my own breathing. When I noticed a tiny point of blue light, I blinked and it grew. The blue light grew as large as a doorway. The chanting stopped.

Téle's voice boomed in my ear. "Tonight we build a bridge to the *saba* of the Romillians of Salantia. As we join our minds together, our hearts guide our thoughts. If your heart guides your thoughts, walk through the door that has opened."

I wanted my heart to guide my thoughts. *How will I know?* I thought wildly. A heartbeat later, I heard Dresa's voice: *It will be so if you intend it.*

Then I forgot to think because the blue light *had* become a door. I went through, head first, as children dive into the wide part of the river on the hottest days of summer.

I felt warmth. Turning toward its source brought me face to face with the *saba*. The women nodded at me. Tu raised his eyebrows. Dresa smiled her secret smile. Téle passed with closed eyes, a thin blue flame emitting from her forehead. I floated. The circle passed before me. I felt for the ground but it was gone.

*Why do you worry so?* Dresa's voice was amused. Then I was staring at a bright multi-colored light coming from dark space. The light became a winged creature. As it approached, copper-colored wings brushed the air, rushing past as a storm rumbles down from the mountain. As the creature slowed, its wings beat faster, causing its body to stand upright in the air.

The flying person was female, with a sternly beautiful face and long hair a shade darker than Dresa's. My heart rattled as I watched this creature alight. Was she in the *saba*? Can everyone see her?

The Romillian walked forward, her wings folding against her back. I gasped when Téle appeared and joined her in the golden circle. She faced the Romillian. Both women bowed.

"The *saba* of our village welcomes Kirith of Salantia, leader of the Romillian people, who flew over our land in peace," Téle said. "We welcome your return in spirit as we meet with you in spirit."

Kirith bowed low. "We welcome you to our *saba*," she replied. "We accept your greetings in spirit as we meet with you in spirit."

I stared at the women, finally realizing that *this* was the *saba*.

"We meet because of your efforts," Kirith said. "We came to your land in response to your desire to know the worlds beyond your world."

"We did not realize our desire for knowledge brought you to us," Téle said.

"Romillians go where we are needed," Kirith said. "We travel to worlds whose inhabitants are ready to open their eyes wider. But as my daughter has told you, we could not survive in your land, so we did not contact you while we lived there. We thought it best not to open a door that led nowhere. I am grateful for this chance to see my beloved daughter again."

"Our effort was successful because Dresa joined her mind to ours," Téle said.

"Where is my daughter?" Kirith asked.

The circle expanded. Into the golden light moved Dresa. She walked slowly, her wings extended. As she entered the circle, Téle stepped back.

I held my breath, watching the winged women face each other. Kirith lifted her arms. Her wings extended. She stepped forward. Dresa walked into her embrace. They pressed themselves against each other, wings quivering. Excitement pulsed through the air. Dresa moved a step away from Kirith and knelt before her mother. Kirith reached down and raised her by the shoulders. They both turned and faced the doorway that Kirith had come through.

A shimmer of light appeared in it. I held my breath. Another being approached the door, wings outstretched. It was smaller than Dresa. As it touched down, it folded its wings.

I knew when I saw the delicate features, gold-flecked hair, and green eyes glistening with tears. My forehead throbbed. Dresa and the newcomer faced each other. They stood motionless, devouring each other with their eyes. Dresa moved first, a firm step with outstretched hands. They embraced, clinging to each other, stroking backs and shoulders.

The love between them was a living force. It burst out of Dresa's body in a stream of bright pink and engulfed Florin. From Florin's chest emitted a burst of pale green that mixed with the pink and filled the space between them. Even I, who know nothing of such matters, felt the great love between them.

Dresa and Florin moved apart and bowed to each other. They vibrated so fast their bodies no longer had clear edges, but became spirals of moving color. As they came together, the vibration increased again until, at the moment they touched, even their faces were moving light. I watched two sparkling columns of light meet, touch, and blend until they were one seething mass of color.

The single spiraling mass of light slowed. Outlines of limbs appeared, then wings. A face formed in the light.

I saw, not Dresa and Florin, not the long-separated daughters of Kirith, but one beautiful woman. She was like Dresa, but not Dresa, so beautiful my throat ached with tears. The twin daughters of Kirith had somehow merged into one exquisite adult.

I wanted to go to her. I wanted her to touch my hand. I wanted her to tell me her secrets. Even Téle, wisest of us all, was a child compared to this shining creature. All this I knew in my heart.

When I called to her in my mind, she turned. Her eyes were as large as our village. I found myself standing on a shore of green water that rippled softly, inviting me to explore the treasure in its depths. *Dresa*, I whispered as I walked into the warm green sea. The water closed over me.

I saw the homeland of the Romillians. Beautiful winged creatures soared through the pastel air, making pictures with their wings. I saw images of forests and waterfalls, of a golden sea where great winged fish soared over waves, of high-domed crystalline structures, of Romillians dancing and laughing, mothers with children, lovers walking on soft grass. Never had I imagined such things, pictures so vibrantly colored and exquisitely wrought, they looked alive.

Soft lyrical tones floated on the wind. I looked for what could be making these sounds. Then I understood. It was the wings of the Romillians. The pictures moved. Breezes swayed the delicate trees, water bubbled over rocks, the waves crashed, and the gentle voices of the Romillians laughed. The pictures had come alive.

*This is my world.* Dresa's voice echoed in my heart. *This is why I must return to my home. Part of me wishes I could stay here with you. But what you see is our art. I was meant to create pictures like these. My heart has always known this. Now that I have joined with Florin, my heart is whole. I will return to my world and make pictures of your land and your people and of you, my brother, so all will know of your strength and kindness. I am not leaving, but returning. Do you understand, Gar?*

How could I not understand? I would have gladly left my home and gone with her if there were a way.

I felt her smile. *I will always remember you.*

The land of the Romillians faded. I floated in the warm green sea.

I awoke in my sleeping place in the darkest part of the night. Nothing stirred except Téle who sat by the open door with her back to me, swaying back and forth as she watched the silent moon sail across the deep dark sky.

∫∫∫

Four summers have passed since Dresa left us. Rain has been plentiful, our village prospers, and Téle has become a grandmother. Our son was born two winters ago, one winter after Mart and I made our household together. I hoped the child would help my mother forget how the *saba* had been when Dresa was with us, for Pel told me that the women could no longer see above the clouds.

Sometimes when Téle looks at me, I see the questions still burning in her eyes.

How could a living person become light? How did Dresa leave us?

I have told her all I could. About the green water, and the land of the Romillians, and the pictures that lived and breathed. But I did not speak about the deep love Dresa had for her twin, nor about the great longing that somehow made possible what happened in the *saba* that night.

Sometimes even now she stares at me as if she is trying to snatch the knowledge straight from my mind.

I want to say, "It was love, Mother, that did it." But these words are not enough. They do not explain what happened that night, and I have no other words that do.

∞

# THE WAY HOME

## Chapter 1

Mata hunched her shoulders against the icy air emanating from the Graylands. It looked even more desolate than she had imagined. The trees were burned sticks, the air thick and foul.

A trickle of a stream at the bottom of a narrow ravine marked the boundary between the Living Forest and the demon's realm, a sagging footbridge her only hope of crossing it. Under her feet grew grass, lush and green, while on the opposite bank was bare dirt. She lifted one foot to step onto the bridge, stopped, and put it back on the grass.

Her long journey had started when Lady Adi appeared in the forest near her village to command her. Mata had been weak with grief from the death of her beloved Sem after the mountain convulsed. In a brief moment, Sem vanished into a crevice that seemed to have no bottom.

On the day of his funeral, the Lady. Mata agreed to make the journey, for what else could she do when the Lady of All appeared in an arc of light in the sacred forest? Mata would do as Adi asked, no matter that she was old and tired, her legs weak, her fingers gnarled.

Now, she had reached the boundary of the Graylands. The presence of the demon chilled her bones. What had made her think she could survive this evil place? None of the priests or hunters who traveled here to challenge the demon had returned. *Eaten by the black sea*, the people whispered.

All the people of the valley, the Caheya, children of Adi, were in danger from the explosions that continued to shake the mountain. Mata thought of her daughter Elem and of little Atarah, the golden one. She raised her chin and stepped onto the rotting wood of the bridge. It creaked under her weight. Clinging with both hands to the frayed ropes, she made her way to the other side.

When she stepped off the bridge, an iciness penetrated her feet. Mata breathed into it, transmuting it with the warmth of her breath. *It won't be that easy*, she thought to the demon.

## Chapter 2

A branch cracks under a human foot. The sound interrupts my dream. I am eager to see what approaches from the lands of the Caheya—surely not more hunters with their puny weapons.

I sense a female presence and draw myself out of the sea. No female has trod my land since the priestess carrying the golden crystal mistook me for one of her kind. I can assume any shape, so it is an easy mistake, but a true priestess would have known better. She was grieving over a missing lover, and I lured her by taking his shape, which I knew since I had devoured him.

I form myself into a shadow and move from one blackened tree stump to another. Her thoughts are faint as a whisper. When I find her, a rush of pleasure seizes me. She is old but she holds herself straight and does not flinch when I appear. Gray and gaunt, dressed in shapeless clothing, she carries a single bundle on her back. I raise myself, like a shadow of the tallest tree, and hiss at her. She freezes. I extend an appendage. Fright vibrates her chest, but she does not move. I encircle her with my darkness.

I speak into her mind. *Why have you come?*

When she answers, she feels soft and pale, like a pure white beach of long-crushed quartz. "I am Mata, sent by Lady Adi, to claim her holy crystal."

Her voice echoes like a note blown on golden trumpets by the harbingers of the gods who have forgotten us. The words don't matter, but I want her voice to continue vibrating through me, for this ragged wretch reminds me of something I have forgotten.

*The crystal is mine. If you turn around now, you may return to your people.*

That is not true, she is too delicious to resist, but I enjoy the sport.

"The crystal has been in our temple for twenty generations," she answers. "It was taken by subterfuge. By the laws that govern all who live, what is stolen must be returned when a clear request is made."

*Is that what you believe you have made? A clear request?*

She stands still as an old tree and stares up at what she believes is my face. I tighten myself around her and squeeze. I am rewarded with the warm sensation that a pool of fear makes as it expands up from her lower parts and seeps into me. As I lap it up, she shivers.

"The crystal belongs to the Goddess." Her voice is strong. "The Living Forest will soon be gone. The rains have stopped. The mountain has exploded once and rumbles still. My people cannot survive here, but without the crystal, they cannot leave. The Caheya will be no use to you when all is a land of shadows."

*But what will I eat?* I ask, oh so softly.

She waits, breathes out her fear, and straightens her shoulders. "You don't need food. You are immortal."

*Liar!*

How could she know what I barely remember? I unwind myself and reform in the shape of the last hunter who came to conquer me. He looked surprised as I swallowed him. The old woman looks surprised that I have released her.

"How long have you lived in this place?" she asks.

*Longer than your bauble sat useless in your temple. The holy Gamani sent me from across the desert mountains to conquer the Caheya and take their land.*

She raises her chin higher. "Adi protects the Caheya."

Her certainty makes me uneasy. *There was a battle.* I should not speak to her, but my silence has gone on too long. *Adi used her power against us. My soldiers perished inside the walls of the city of the Caheya. Your bitch goddess massacred us.*

"The Lady doesn't intervene in human affairs. She persuades."

*Then she persuaded the high priestess to massacre us. Her power was like nothing we had seen. She used no weapon. Yet my men and their horses died in agony.*

"N'ta."

As she utters the word, the old one shrinks. "The power is called N'ta. For protection. The Zhitigal could not bear its highest notes and so it killed them. It has not been used in battle since that time."

For all the centuries I have pondered that battle, I never considered that my soldiers had been murdered by sound alone.

"It is a science of our people, used to protect us from intruders. The weapons of the Zhitigal penetrated the shield the N'ta formed around our villages. They killed our cattle as they grazed. Before then, nothing had ever penetrated the N'ta. We were forced to seek a way to increase its power. Only when all negotiations failed was it used."

*Tell that to those who died.*

"It is said that many survived and returned to their homeland."

*You know your history, old woman.*

"The temple records tell the history of the Caheya. They tell how you came here."

I notice that I have retreated from her, and push myself forward. *I do not give up. I do not withdraw like the coward Gamani, the god of the Zhitigal who gave me immortality for my efforts on his behalf. He returned to his palace in the sky and left me to Adi who trapped me in this miserable barren land.*

*There is no escape for me as long as your Goddess rules. But now that I have the crystal, more of your kind come seeking it. I have enjoyed many meals because of that crystal, and more will come after you have gone.*

"Will you eat me?"

Her voice reminds me that once I was more than a shadow in a black sea.

An image of a silver flame so bright it could light a whole world erupts from my memory. It hangs in the air, leaving me weak with longing. I force myself to answer her: *I eat everything that lives, but before you die, you may see your crystal. It is in my sea.*

She wants the crystal more than she fears me and follows me out of the wood to the field of lava rocks. While she picks her way across the rocks, she lets down her guard.

I enter her mind and from there, I know the sea as she knows it: thick and black, viscous, heaving. The sucking sounds of the deep waves bubbling to the surface are like music. I am entranced by the sharpness of her perceptions, how clearly separate are each rock and stump. I had forgotten why I stayed with the other priestess so long before I ate her, but now I remember. I stayed for this exquisite perception.

When the old one notices where I am, she blows me out of her mind with a single exhale. Again, I am a shadow among shadows.

"Bring me the crystal." She stands erect and gray against the black rocks.

*You must come for it.*

I move into the sea and stretch myself on its surface. The waves ripple through me. I look back and see the old woman. I curl myself into a wave and hurl myself at the shore. I wet her boots. She does not move. I pretend to be the crystal calling to her. *I am here. Take me home. I belong with you.*

She lets her bundle fall. She raises both hands, as if seeking justice from above.

Then, slowly—so slowly I hold my breath—she takes one step, then another, toward me.

As she walks into my sea, the waves rush toward her like devouring mouths. They tug at her skirt. I hear her thoughts, feel her fear that the boiling water will scorch her skin, and then her relief when she discovers it is cold.

More fear erupts as her feet go numb. When the water reaches her chest, she takes two steps with arms raised, stops, and reaches higher. She speaks in a language I have never heard. The waves cease their sucking. They fall back. She takes another step. The water retreats. The old woman sings an ancient song of power that frightens my sea. I float on its surface, beyond her reach, and watch as she walks forward on her frozen feet.

When the crystal answers, the sound makes me wish I remembered how to cry.

Instead, I bellow across the water.

She does not notice. She looks down. I follow her gaze. A tunnel of pale light forms under the surface. She lowers herself and swims toward it. The crystal I have kept imprisoned all these years has answered the old woman's call. Buried for centuries in an underground cave, it sends out a beam of light to search for her.

I scream at the sea to devour her. *Now! Take her! Eat her! Dissolve her flesh and then dissolve her bones.*

She lifts one arm, pushes it through the water, and propels herself forward. The sea hangs motionless. Never have I felt such stillness. Never have I seen a living creature survive immersion in my sea for so long. Yet the wrinkled old hag swims.

The golden crystal emits a column of light whose beauty I cannot bear. I try to lift myself from the sea and take another form, but I am immobilized by a force I do not understand.

*Do it!* I scream to the sea that has never before refused my command. *Take her. Kill her.*

The sea moans, an eerie wail. It pulls at her soaked rags, forcing her deeper. She goes down into its black depths, but the column of golden light has reached her. She swims into it. She moves toward the cave that can be entered only from the sea. She comes to the mouth of the cave with its jagged rocks as sharp as glass, protected by the tunnel of golden light and disappears inside. The light dims. The sea begins to rock.

*Too late! The crystal protects her. What good are you if you cannot kill one frail human?*

The sea erupts with angry waves that toss me about until I notice I can move again and reform myself into a thundercloud. I look down at the boiling water and imagine the old one impaled on the lava rocks that line the cave.

I could have eaten her while she stood on the shore. Now it may be too late. I shake myself until a clap of thunder pours out of me. I am uncertain. And very curious.

## Chapter 3

Mata grabbed onto a large rock and hoisted herself out of the rushing water. She clung there, panting. When the next wave lifted her, she scrambled into the upper chamber of the cave, a space wide enough to lie flat. It was full of sand and sharp rocks, but safe from the water below.

Drawn by the vibration of the crystal, she dug in the sand until she uncovered it, unblemished by long years buried. Round and glowing with life, it hummed louder when she wiped away the sand with the frayed hem of her skirt.

"You are safe now," she whispered. "You can fulfill your destiny. You will save the Caheya. Now I must wrap you tightly and bind you to me so you will be safe. I hope you don't mind."

She tore strips from her tattered skirt. She placed the crystal in the soft leather pouch she wore around her neck, fastened with a silver chain so long it dangled at her waist. When the crystal was safely inside the pouch, she pulled tight the pouch's leather straps and wrapped the strips of cloth through its loops. Last, she fastened the cloth strips twice around her waist and tied them securely. No one could remove it from her body as long as she lived.

She collapsed on the sand. She was in a cave which extended into a narrow tunnel that dissolved into blackness. A shaft of light shone from an opening far over her head. If the tunnel led to the surface, there might be a way out without going back into the sea.

A voice in her head hissed. *Hopeless.*

Mata knew that voice. It had drawn her into the black sea. She had surprised it by surviving the water.

She could not feel her feet. She looked down, expecting to see them rotted to stumps by the black water, but, although shriveled and naked, they were intact. How long had she been in the sea? Minutes might have passed. Or days. No point in trying to work it out. All that mattered was getting out of this cave.

*Stay and rest,* the voice crooned. *You have suffered. You deserve rest.*

She tore more strips from her skirt and bound her feet. Then she wrapped strips of cloth around her knees and elbows. "We will get out," she said to the crystal.

Leaning on a rock, she climbed to her feet and took one step toward the tunnel. She fell. A rock grazed her cheek. She wiped blood from her face and hoisted herself up. She walked into the tunnel. If it did not lead to the surface, her people would never reach the new land of Adi's promise.

The tunnel reeked of rotted flesh. She tripped on a pile of bones. Farther on, she found a desiccated tree limb that she used to tap the sides of the cave.

Sometimes light appeared from holes above and the tunnel looked the same each time—black rocks, patches of sand, piles of bones, nothing alive. She forged on, slow and dogged, and rounded a sharp curve to find a pile of boulders blocking the way. At the top of the pile was an opening to the surface.

She sank onto the sand and closed her eyes. Her mind filled with images of the stream that offered its water for her village and the fertile fields that provided food in the days before the summers grew too hot. She felt the cool breezes from the mountain and smelled the sweetness of fresh-picked corn. Mata forced her eyes open. Those days were gone.

The pile of jagged black boulders stretched to the top of the tunnel. She could climb over them if she went slowly. She could squeeze through the opening. Of course she could. But if she did not find water soon, none of it would matter.

She began the slow, laborious climb over the rocks. Sharp edges tore her flesh. When she reached the top, blood was running from new cuts in her hands and feet. The hole was not large enough for her shoulders to pass through, so she pulled at the smallest rocks. When they came loose, she threw them down and used her bleeding fingers to scrape away loose dirt. She clawed and scraped and pulled at rocks and dirt until the hole was large enough to push through.

A breath of air energized her. Mata pushed upward until she was free to the waist. She grabbed onto a log and pulled her body out of the tunnel. She emerged in a small clearing surrounded by trees, well into the forest, out of reach of the venomous sea.

At nightfall, she came to a pool of stagnant water near a grove of blackened pine trees. She fell to the ground to drink and thanked Adi that she would live another day. She slept where she had fallen, hands clasped over her waist where the crystal hummed, and dreamed of crystal castles glowing silver under an azure sky.

The journey through the forest of the Graylands to the sea had taken two days when she had full use of her legs. Now, she hobbled painfully from one tree to the next. The way back loomed before her.

The voice in her head crooned. *Too long. Stay here. Rest.*

"Quiet," she said and hobbled on. Days went by, all the same. When she came to the little stream she had followed when she entered the Graylands, it remembered her and offered itself so she could wash away the black filth that clung to her skin and clothing. Without asking her name, the stream called her Matani, the word for grandmother in the old language. The word reminded her of Atarah.

*I'm coming,* she thought to her golden-haired granddaughter, the only child born with such coloring that anyone in the valley could remember. Her skin was like pale cream and even her eyes had a glint of gold in their amber depths. On Mata's last night in the village, her daughter Elem had begged her not to leave.

"Atarah needs you," Elem said.

The child had looked up with those strange pale eyes and smiled. "You will come back for me," she said when her mother turned away, and Mata had hugged her so tightly the child squirmed in her arms.

Mata prayed for sunlight but thick gray clouds hung low and motionless. No birds chattered. No animals scurried in the underbrush. She walked past thickets of brambles and stunted bushes. She found edible berries and tiny mushrooms. The buzzing of the voice continued in her mind, but she no longer heard the words.

When she came to the meadow marking the boundary between the Graylands and the Living Forest, Mata sank to her knees beside the stream and wept. She had brought the crystal to the land of the Caheya.

The voice rumbled. *You are alone. No one waits. If you go on, you will die on the trail. Stay and rest. It is pleasant here by the stream.*

Mata wanted only to stretch out by the stream and sleep. Instead, she crawled to her feet, stamped her walking stick against the ground once, and trudged across the rickety bridge into the meadow of the Living Forest.

146

*I'm coming,* she thought, to her daughter, to the golden child, to all who awaited her.

*You will never see them again. Rest here. I will make your passage easy and painless.*

"Go back to your sea," Mata told the voice. "You are not wanted in the land of the living."

## Chapter 4

The living forest was not as lush as she remembered. The ground was covered with a thin layer of white ash and many trees were blackened. Mata felt for the crystal at her waist. It vibrated through its filthy wrappings and reassured her that she was in the right place.

She searched for the path that would take her over the mountain and down into the valley of the Caheya, but the white stuff covered everything. A distant rumble sounded. Deep below the surface, the ground shook. The eastern mountain must have erupted again while she was in the Graylands, and with a great force for ash and coals to have come this far.

"We must hurry," she said to the crystal.

She slogged through ash, foraging for food, finding little of substance, but enough to keep her alive. On the third day, she climbed over a bare rock hill and down a steep slope into a clearing where three antelope stopped snuffling for roots to stare at her with hollow eyes.

*They are food*, said the voice.

"No."

*You will die if you do not eat more. Eating will save your people.*

"The animals are my companions." But she thought of how much faster she could walk if her belly were full.

As if they heard her, two of the antelopes raised their heads, wheeled and trotted away.

Mata sat on a granite rock near the remaining antelope. She had never eaten animal flesh except for a ritual taste of the wild bull the hunters killed each year for the spring festival. Before the drought, the hunters used to bring meat for the people all year long, but Mata had kept her ancient vow to eat no flesh.

"Are you sick?" she asked the antelope. "Is that why you offer yourself?"

The animal lowered its head as if it were looking for a mouthful of forage, but its soft lips lingered above the ground. *I will lie down for you. I am no sicker than the others, but none will survive if you do not open the gate so the bridge can form. I offer myself for the sake of my people.*

*Easy prey*, the voice cackled.

Mata looked into the antelope's brown eyes. "I may be dying, but I will not take your life to save my own. If I reach my village in time, your people can cross with us. If the bridge forms, all will cross."

The antelope raised its head and shook it twice. *You keep Her ways. It is noted.*

With a flick of its tail, it bounded away.

*Foolish hag.*

"I will survive without losing who I am."

As the voice laughed, Mata remembered the sucking sound of the waves of the inland sea.

The days grew shorter. The air cooled, bringing relief from the heat of the ash but then snow fell. The ground froze. Twice she lost the trail and had to retrace her steps. One morning, she awoke to find snow covering her. She was content in her bundle, curled in on herself. The crystal on her chest kept her warm, but if she didn't move soon, she would not be able to rise. She tried to flex one leg. Nothing happened.

*Rest now. All will be well. You have fought long. I will care for you.*

"You bring death." She kicked her right foot. It moved an inch. She kicked her left foot. Pain shot through her knee. She uncurled her right hand and grasped a fallen tree limb. She used the limb to hoist herself to a sitting position. She gasped with effort. Still, her legs did not move. When she could breathe normally, she tried again to rise, but fell back against a rock. She fingered the crystal through its wrappings.

"Lady, help me. I cannot rise. Help your daughter who wishes only to fulfill her purpose."

An owl hooted a warning.

"I know there's danger," she said.

With her hands, Mata stretched out her legs, hoping to warm them with the movement. They did not respond to her commands. For the first time, she doubted her ability to complete her sacred mission. Perhaps the voice was right.

As soon as that thought settled in her mind, a sharp pain shot through the top of her head. She gasped and fell forward. Colors vibrated and shattered before her eyes, forming rainbows that coalesced into an ocean of color, bathing her in beauty. Too much beauty, but she would not be fooled by ephemeral visions. She screwed up her eyes and willed that when she opened them, she would see only the forest. Slowly, her vision cleared.

A shadowy figure, human-shaped but indistinct at the edges, peered out from behind a tree just beyond her reach. He was dressed in black, his large head bare, face sickly pale, with smudges for eyes. He disappeared behind the tree.

The voice had moved out of her and taken the form of a man.

Mata pushed her legs from side to side, struggling to rise. She dragged herself to a sturdy tree and used it to pull herself upright.

Laughter rose into the frosty air.

"No," Mata screamed. She took a step, lost her balance, and fell. Lifting her face from the muddy snow, she said, "No" again. She couldn't see the shadow figure, but it was there, waiting. She lay panting, one hand on the crystal at her waist, the other grasping a sharp rock.

The shadow figure reappeared. He started for her, walking through the snow, one slow step at a time. As he walked, a horrible smile stretched his mouth. He was above her.

She gripped her rock.

He looked down. She gasped, for beneath the dark smudges of eyebrows, his eyes shone an eerie unearthly blue.

Suddenly the forest erupted into sound. The owl hooted again, a series of urgent screeches. A flock of birds rose into the air, chattering loudly. A deer streaked across the snow. A crashing sound came from behind a dense thicket near Mata's head. Something large was moving toward her. Moving fast.

The dark figure ran. Mata turned toward the new danger. A bellow rose from the thicket. An animal burst into the open. She ducked. A bull? A boar? It headed straight for her, hooves thundering. "Lady, preserve me," Mata whispered into the snow.

The creature thundered toward her head. It stopped abruptly, spraying dirt and small stones in all directions where its hooves tore through the layer of snow.

She raised her head to see what was about to trample her. The animal tossed its fine-boned head, pale gray with a darker stripe down its nose and a mane whiter than the snow covering her.

"You're a horse," she breathed. "A beautiful horse."

The horse lifted his head and loosed a ferocious sound into the cold air. He lowered his muzzle to Mata and snuffled at her back.

*It's all right now,* the horse said into her mind. He stamped one foot. *There was a demon lurking, but he has fled. You have come far, old woman, but it is still a long way to your village.*

"Who are you? How did you find me?"

*The antelope you spared sent the call. Lady Adi instructed me to find you. We are only three days from your village if you ride on my back.*

"I thought I would be food for that demon."

*Not today.*

"Riding one like you seems against nature, but since I can no longer walk, I accept your kind offer."

The horse pushed his nose against her chest. *I am Caelestis. Use the straps hanging from my pack to pull yourself up.*

"I am Mata. Lady Adi sent me to the Graylands and now I bear the golden crystal of the Caheya."

*I know who you are. The memory of the Living Forest is long.*

Caelestis positioned himself close to Mata. She grasped the straps of his pack with both hands. The horse stepped backward, one cautious step, then another. His movement

153

gave her enough momentum to regain her feet. She leaned against his warm neck.

*There are nuts and dried fruit in my pack. Eat, and then we will be off.*

Mata unfastened the leather bag and took out a piece of dried apple. "Where did you get the pack? All this food?"

*The Lady provides. Her lemurs filled the pack and secured it to me.*

She was surprised at the mention of lemurs. "I did not know any survived in our land."

*A few still live in underground caves.* Caelestis blew his warm breath on her face. He rubbed his nose against her chest. *Eat your fill and drink from the pouch. Then find a rock to stand on so you can reach my back. We can cover many miles yet today.*

She looked up at the gray sky. "There may be no moonlight."

Caelestis snorted. *My path is lighted from within, as is yours.*

"What do you know of my path?"

*Much is known to those who serve the Lady.*

After she had eaten and drunk, Mata pulled herself onto his back.

*Hold on.*

Caelestis stretched out his long neck. Mata fastened one hand around the strap and grabbed his mane with the other. The horse started down the trail in a canter, an easy rocking gait. As she grew accustomed to his rhythm, he moved faster. Soon the bleak landscape was flowing past.

## Chapter 5

The cursed horse! The hag would have been mine. She was easy prey as she lay in the snow, clutching her rock. As if such a thing could be a weapon against me. I could easily devour her, for I am ruler of the Graylands, beloved of Gamani, adversary of Adi.

Yet one old woman eludes me. Without the wretched horse, I could have taken my time. Already the taste of her watered my mouth. The meal was so close, and then snatched away by a beloved of Adi, one of the few creatures in this land too pure of mind to be penetrated by my wiles. As long as the old woman stays with the horse, she is untouchable.

I have left her mind. Without another host, I must return to my realm, for my shadow body cannot long survive in the Living Forest. I do not give up. I will go on. I will have this old woman who knows too much. When I have devoured her, there will be nothing left to remind me of my weakness. Somewhere in this forest walks a creature I can take. I will enter it. I will track her. I will find her. She will be mine.

∫∫∫

Caelestis and Mata traveled well past sunset. The clouds had parted and the moon was high when they stopped at a small cave near a spring. When Mata tried to dismount, she found she could not move. Caelestis carried her into the cave and lowered himself to the ground. Mata rolled off him onto a pile of dead leaves. Caelestis rose and nudged her with his muzzle.

*Get up and make a fire. There is plenty of wood within reach. Use your powers to make a spark.*

Mata hauled herself up against the nearest wall of the cave. "I have no powers."

Caelestis pushed a couple of dry sticks toward her with his nose. *It's too late to pretend you are not high priestess of Adi.*

"You are mistaken."

*The goddess would not choose an emissary unable to walk the required path.*

Mata looked at him for a long moment. She nodded and gathered sticks into a pile. She leaned over them and blew onto the pile. Forming a picture of a campfire in her mind, she blew on them again. A spark erupted and caught the ragged edge of a small twig. Mata cupped her hand around the pile and blew gently a third time. A flame appeared.

Caelestis bobbed his head. *Take more food from my pack. A stream is close. You must refill the water pouch yourself.*

Mata reached for the larger tree limbs the horse had pushed toward her and fed the fire. "The warmth is good."

Caelestis settled down beside her. She reached for his pack and extracted dried apple and some nuts. "Do you need to graze?"

*Later. When you have eaten, lie next to me. My warmth will help you sleep. We leave at dawn, priestess.*

"You are a good companion, horse."

*I promised Lady Adi to bring you safely to your village. Much is at stake.*

Mata wanted to say something else, but she could not remember the words she wanted to use before her eyes closed.

Dawn found them moving through the woods, the old woman clinging to the horse's neck, the horse moving through a thick forest of brambles and looming bushes. They rode all day and camped at dusk near the hollow of a burned-out tree in a small meadow. After she had eaten and drunk, Mata lay on a patch of grass and looked up at the sky.

"It's long since I saw stars."

Caelestis raised his head from the grass. *The sky is seldom so clear. I have heard nothing from the mountain since we came together.*

"Is that an omen?"

He snorted and went back to his patch of grass.

Mata decided that, omen or not, she would stay awake to watch the stars circle the heavens. After a time, two squirrels dashed up to her with their cheeks bulging. They stopped just out of reach and sat on their haunches. She nodded to them.

*I sent them to look for more nuts for you,* Caelestis said. *Take them if you wish.*

She realized the squirrels were waiting for a sign. "Thank you for your gift."

The squirrels dropped to four legs and deposited their stash of redburry nuts in a pile. They were succulent and meaty and grew too high in their trees for her to reach.

She poured water over them from her pouch and bit into one.

"Delicious," she said to the squirrels.

The squirrels chattered to each other. They fell silent and stared at her with tiny black eyes.

"The food is most welcome," she said.

The squirrels turned and scampered away.

"That was kind. I hope their families are not deprived."

*If you are not successful, it will not matter. Go to sleep, priestess. We start again at dawn.*

The next day Caelestis kept a faster pace even though they traveled up a steep incline. They came to patches of snow, some as high as the horse's forelegs, and there he went slowly, careful not to jostle his passenger.

Mata shivered with the cold. "How far up must we go?"

*Soon we reach the summit. Then we go down the other side of the mountain that overlooks your village. I know a cave we can shelter in tonight. Then we have only a day's ride to your home.*

"Bless you." Mata hunched her shoulders against the cold and leaned closer to the horse's warm neck.

They reached the cave just after the moon rose, so there was enough light for Mata to gather wood for a fire. She rummaged in the pack and brought out the last of the dried apple. She imagined the tiny lemur hands that had placed it there and thanked them silently for their kindness.

"It's been a long journey," she said to Caelestis. "Without you, I would have died in the snow."

He blinked his large brown eyes. *As long as you have lived, why do you think snow would kill you now?*

Mata stepped back. The rough wall of the cave scraped her shoulders. "What did the Lady tell you?"

*That you are the only human who could retrieve the crystal. That you needed help getting through the forest.* Caelestis touched his nose to her shoulder. *Your journey has been longer than any human knows, priestess. You have concealed yourself well.*

"Nothing but the crystal has been concealed. I journeyed to the Graylands because the Lady Adi required it. Now I bring the crystal to my village, for only human hands can make the magic needed to open the gate concealed within it. I am only a messenger."

*Did you know that the animals who follow the Goddess remember every lifetime we have lived, even to the beginning of our time in this land?*

Mata's knees trembled. She sank down in the sand. "How far back do you remember, Caelestis?"

*Since before the time of the great battle.*

She picked up a stick and poked at the fire. "You have been reborn many times."

*All have been reborn many times. The cycles of life and rebirth come more frequently than before.*

"I know nothing of that."

*You lie to one who remembers you as the High Priestess of your people, most beloved of Adi.*

"No."

*You lie to one who remembers that you chose to fight the intruders against the will of the Goddess.*

"Stop."

*You lie to one who saw the battle and lost his life because of it.*

Mata sprang to her feet, brandishing a flaming branch in her hand. She raised the torch. Shadows moved across the wall of the cave. "Stop! That is ancient history. Even if I did live then, I have no memory of it."

*You lie to one who remembers your face.*

She threw down the flaming branch in the space between them.

"Everyone would have died!" she cried. "If I had not fought, they would have been slaughtered. Do you understand? Everyone. I had no choice. The powers were there, in my hand. How could I not use them to save the people?"

She remembered the agony of that day, when she stood on the upper wall of the temple in the city of Catala and watched the Zhitigal soldiers crowd into the courtyard below. Their armor had glistened in the light of the rising sun as the breath of their fighting horses rose like puffs of smoke in the cold air.

She sank to her knees and bowed her head. "I was called Matara then," she whispered.

Caelestis rubbed his soft nose against the top of her head.

## Chapter 6

The air blew cold against Matara's face as first light crept over the mountain. Under moonlight, armored men had rammed open the wooden gates of the city. Meant only to keep domestic animals from wandering, the gates fell easily.

The reverberation of crashing logs and splintering wood had driven the Caheya to hiding places inside their homes or through secret passageways in the outer walls to seek shelter in the buildings scattered over the farmlands.

Now the courtyard of the Temple of Adi was overrun with Zhitigal astride their warhorses, men and beasts encased in shining battle regalia, waiting in silent rows for a command from their leader.

Matara stood on the upper terrace of the temple and looked down at the courtyard through a round hole in the mud brick wall. She did not see Kai, the warrior-priest who led the Zhitigal. He must be with the larger number of soldiers outside the city gates. He would give the signal to attack, but would not be caught in the trap. She thanked Adi for this small favor.

Only a few hours before Kai had stood in her private chamber, shaking his head as if he were in pain as, once again, she refused to name him High Priest of the Caheya.

163

"Lady Adi protects the Caheya," she said, pressing his rough hand with hers. "Neither she nor I can accept sharing rule with your god Gamani. We are people of peace. There is plenty of game in the forest and enough farmland for all. We will share what we have. Kai, on behalf of my people, I beg you not to use your weapons against us. Nothing good will come from a war."

He touched his lips to her long brown fingers. His face softened. "We have discussed this every evening since my men pitched camp outside your walls and all we do is talk in circles. You are stubborn, Matara. Is it not better for your people to live with Gamani than die for Adi?"

She pulled away her hands. "We will die if we must."

He grabbed her shoulders. "Don't make me slaughter defenseless innocents. You have no weapons save the knives you use for hunting. You stand no chance. Please, Matara, listen to me."

She ignored the tremors in her body where he touched her. "Go and leave us in peace."

"I cannot."

"You fear to displease your god."

He made an angry sound. "Is that what you believe?"

She was silent.

"Matara, listen. Together we can rule the Caheya and the Zhitigal. Your life will change little. Is that not better than to die like an animal in a pen?" He gripped her so tightly she pulled out of his grasp.

"The Caheya obey Adi. We live in harmony with all creatures. If I agree to what you ask, all that will change. Am I wrong?"

His lips tightened. "Some things must change. But is life not better than death? We could be together. Make me your priest and my soldiers will not enter your gates."

She looked into his eyes. "I cannot."

His strange blue eyes turned as dark as a summer thundercloud. His jaw clenched as his hands dropped to his sides.

She stepped back.

He whirled and strode toward the door, his heavy boots pounding the bare floor. The slam of the wooden door reverberated through Matara's spine.

That had been hours ago. Now Matara felt the holy ones of Adi leaving their chambers and gathering behind her. They were the eldest of the temple, the priests and priestesses who were her closest companions and advisors, the ones with the power to summon N'ta.

"Matara, it is time to decide."

She didn't have to turn to know who spoke. Tena, her closest friend, spoke for those who wanted her to use N'ta, the highest power known to the servants of Adi. It would stop the Zhitigal, but what else it might do she was not certain.

"If we use it, they will all die. This is not the simple song we used to protect our cattle." Matara said. "Even though they mean to murder us, we are sworn to do no harm."

"Adi will forgive us," said Benus. "We cannot allow the people to be murdered in their homes."

Reni's voice was clear and strong. "If we die, we return to Adi. We will begin again in a new place. Remember, we are Caheya."

Matara turned to look at Jac, the eldest living priestess of Adi. The old woman stood straight, her dark eyes sparking with passion. "Yes, we are Caheya, but never have we faced such barbarity. We saw how their weapon ripped through the animal enclosure and tore open the bodies of the cattle. That is what they will do to every person in Catala if we don't defend ourselves. This new danger calls for a new response. Adi gave us brains so we can think of our own solutions."

"Can you talk to their leader again?" asked Clem, the youngest.

"I have talked and talked. It is no use."

"They have broken down the walls," said Benus. "They wait for the command to break into the Temple. Matara must decide now."

Matara looked at their drawn faces, the strain of the last weeks etched deep on every one. "You are all good people. I know you are not of one mind. The people are not of one mind. I thought we could reach understanding with the invaders. I didn't think they would slaughter us if they came to know us. But their god has no mercy in his heart."

"Whatever you decide, we are with you," Jac said. "If you say not to fight, give us time to return to our families so we can die with them. If you choose to fight, we will join our voices with yours in the highest song of the N'ta.

Tears ran down Matara's cheeks. "You are all beloved of Adi."

She turned from them and pressed her face against the rough surface of the wall. More soldiers were coming in the gate from the fields beyond, the horses pressed close against each so they looked like a solid mass of armor and restless legs. The men brandished gleaming long swords. Some had strung bows with long arrows and aimed them at the temple. Horses had pulled inside the gate a platform on wheels that held a large metal object with a protruding part that Matara knew would emit something merciless.

*Kai,* she commanded silently. His face appeared in her inner vision.

*Beloved,* he said. Then he closed his fierce thunder blue eyes against her.

Matara's breath caught. She opened her eyes and drew herself up to her full height, which was more than twice the size of her physical body. Below, two soldiers noticed the huge figure that suddenly appeared at the top of the wall. They shouted to their companions. They waved swords. They pointed arrows at her. She felt the power of Adi coursing through her blood, into her hands and throat, filling her lungs.

"Adi, forgive me," she whispered. Then, loudly, so all the courtyard could hear, she cried, "The Caheya do not die this day."

At her command, all the beloveds of Adi assumed their full heights. From afar, it seemed like an army of giants had appeared from nowhere. They moved close to Matara, pressing against her and each other like a mass of brown-robed giants with gleaming faces staring out of voluminous hoods.

"Sing!" Matara commanded.

As one, the holy ones of Adi opened their mouths. Out came the first notes of the N'ta, the song of containment. The song rose on the morning air, swelling louder and higher. It formed a circle of energy around the invaders that none could see but those who guided it.

The horses felt its power first. Many reared straight up into the air, trying to escape the relentless sound that pierced their sensitive ears. The beloved of Adi sang louder and faster. They chanted the holy sounds meant to protect them from danger. The energy of N'ta completed the circle around the Zhitigal who had breached the walls of the city.

When the circle was complete, all the horses went wild, but there was nowhere for them to go. A few at the rear tried to bolt out through the ruined gates, toward the rest of the Zhitigal who waited down the hill, but running into a fence of N'ta is like running into an invisible wall of stone. The horses screamed and fell, crushing their riders.

When the circle was complete, the N'ta continued its work of containment. Its task was to protect by enclosing. As the voices chanted the final tones of the song, the energy of the song filled in the space above the Zhitigal and below them so the invaders were enclosed in a huge circle of light vibrating at a speed so high that men and beasts alike felt they were being torn apart by invisible weapons. This happened only in their minds. Their bodies were whole as they fell lifeless in the courtyard, suffocated from the depletion of air within the circle.

The weakest fell first, gasping and clutching their chests. To the robed ones watching from above, it took a long time for the men and beasts to cease their struggles. To the Caheya watching from their secret hiding places, it took only moments for the N'ta to save them from destruction.

## Chapter 7

Mata looked into the embers of the fire as if her salvation were hiding in the coals.

"They all died. We arranged them in respectful rows, men and beasts, and lit a pyre. We burned down the breached walls and the outer row of storehouses. The soldiers who had stayed outside the walls turned and ran."

Caelestis nudged her back. *I remember, priestess. The Zhitigal captured me on their march through the valley. They bound me by the head and forced me to carry their supplies. Before the battle, I made several trips between your storehouses and the Zhitigal's camp.*

"It was then you saw me," Mata said in wonder. She shook her head as if to dispel a memory. "We gave them food during the days they camped outside the walls, while I talked with Kai."

*I carried that food. I was lucky to be in the far camp when the battle began. To the Zhitigal outside the walls, it seemed like a great magic had taken their first guard. They turned and fled without order or discipline. They flew through the valley, into the forest, and around the great inland sea, barely stopping to rest. They lost many animals in the flight though the desert. When they straggled into the camp where they had left their women and children with a few warriors to protect them, they looked for their leader among the survivors. They could not find Kai. You know the rest.*

Mata nodded. She wanted to rise and stretch, but she could not feel her legs.

"What happened to you then?"

Caelestis blew his warm breath on her numb legs. *At the camp, they put me in an enclosure for horses. I broke through the fence and escaped, but in the stampede that followed I was thrown to the ground and broke a leg. I died the next day.*

Mata shivered. "I didn't think he would attack. Not until the last day did I believe it would happen. Forgive me, Caelestis, for your death, and all the senseless deaths I caused that day."

He rested his muzzle on her shoulder. *I judge no one who speaks the truth. It is a great temptation to break this rule of the Goddess. Especially when death is the alternative.*

"What is it you seek now, horse?"

He pawed the ground. *I am a steward of the Lady. I grieve for your pain.*

She stroked the soft hair between his ears as she looked into the fire and saw again the burning bodies of the intruders.

"After I used the N'ta to repel the invaders, we rebuilt the city. Life resumed, and much was as it had been. But the unity we had enjoyed with ourselves and the Lady was gone. We had broken the covenant of the Goddess, to harm no one, and every Caheya knew it. No one blamed me. Most praised my actions.

But as time went on, I heard tales about how hard everyday tasks had become. Fewer babies were born. Fewer came to study at the temple. Crops failed. Adi had not withdrawn from us. She is the Goddess who loves all. She does not judge, but my actions weakened our connection to her. We were less than we had been.

"After many years, I realized I was aging so slowly it was as if I had become an immortal. There was no explanation for it and I asked for none. I lived with the results of my folly day after day, year after endless year.

"Later, the city fell into disrepair, for the people were no longer of one vision. We had built our houses close, each touching its neighbor, for we wanted the pleasure of being close to our relatives. When the crops failed, that changed. A desire for separateness came over the people. Groups went off and formed villages. After two generations, no one lived in the city. There was nothing to keep the holy ones of Adi in their deserted temple, so they too went to the villages, most to where their families lived, but some joined villages that had no holy one, so every village had a small temple and a *saba* for performing the rituals. It came to seem natural to live apart from each other.

"I went with my family, but as everyone aged and died, I remained the same. No one mentioned it, for all feared me, which was the hardest to bear. One day I left my village and went to live alone in the wilderness until all who had known me were gone. Then I came back with a different name and joined another village. I have done this many times. This last time I dared to marry and have a child. When my husband died in the first explosion of the mountain, I knew the time of reckoning had come.

"When the Lady told me to go to the Graylands to retrieve the crystal, I knew I was the only one who might survive the journey. But when she said that the Graylands would accelerate my aging, I was happy, for I would do anything to save my people and end the torture of an endless life."

*So death is what you seek.*

"I am content to be reborn as the Lady sees fit."

They watched the fire throw shadows on the wall of the cave.

Mata lowered her head to her knees. "After the battle, when Adi ordered the dividing, and the Graylands were created as a boundary between the Caheya and the Zhitigal, we lost our chance to continue growing in wisdom. We could only go backward. That is my fault. Is that the confession you seek from me, horse?"

Caelestis lowered his head and moved his velvet lips over the edge of her skirt. *Only truth opens the way.*

Mata shook her head. "If truth can be found. Tell me, will I succeed in this task? Have you foresight in this matter?"

*I know only what has gone before. The future I leave to Adi. You are brave, priestess, to make this attempt.*

"Now that you know my truth, will you take me the rest of the way?"

*I came here knowing you. And I know that desire blinded you all those lifetimes ago. It caused you to make war on the one you loved because he betrayed you.*

"No! That is not the reason!" Mata rose and grabbed his mane with both hands. "Kai marched against my people. He cared nothing for life. He cared nothing for children and the land and the animals and the great love that flourishes when all are respected. He was ready to murder us all to show his god that he was the most powerful of warriors. That proved he did not love me."

She stopped as the awful realization flowed through her. Tears filled her throat. She choked. Fell to her knees. Her forehead scraped the ground. A desperate sound came out of her. She looked up at Caelestis with hollow eyes. "That's what you came to tell me? I led my people to ruin because I was spurned?"

Caelestis rested his muzzle on her head. *How can we learn what love is if we do not follow where it takes us?*

"It has brought me here," she whispered. "Can that be enough?"

*Come, old woman. You could not change his nature any more than he could change yours. You have both suffered for your actions. No matter the past, a new day is coming. I will carry you to your village. If we all play our parts, the Lady's gate will open. The rest will be washed away in the new land.*

When Caelestis went out to forage, Mata curled into a ball by the fire, and pulled her rags around her. Her mind was empty, her body numb. She listened to the dying embers of the fire crackling in the darkness, and when she slept, she dreamed of strange blue eyes and the screams of horses.

♪♪♪

As first light filtered through the trees, they set out, but had gone only a few miles when a roar in the distance startled them both.

Caelestis stopped short. *The mountain.*

"Go, horse," Mata said. "Time is short." The trail wound through meadows that looked familiar to her, and when they pushed through a thick stand of brush into a small clearing, Mata told him to stop. "This is the place where Adi gave me my task."

*Your village is near. Down that trail.*

"Leave me here. I would like to sit and gather myself before I go down."

175

His ears pricked forward. *I won't leave you in the wilderness.*

"I know the way, horse."

Another roar.

*The explosion is near. I fear for my herd. I left them in the forest.*

"You must find them."

*They were to head south if conditions worsened.*

Mata slid off his back. "I give thanks to the Lady and all her companions. But most I thank you for your strong back and wisdom. Your family waits for you. Go lead them to safety. I will stay here and prepare myself. I am stronger now. It will be good to walk down the old path for the last time." Mata stroked his neck. "I will miss you."

He snorted and stamped a front foot. *If you are going, remove the leather straps from my back.*

She unstrapped the food bag and slung it over her shoulder. "I have had no braver a companion."

He pushed his nose against her sleeve. *If you succeed, we may meet again.*

Mata scratched the soft spot between his ears. "Safe passage for all your family."

Caelestis snorted and raised his head to thunder his call that his task was complete. She stepped back as he spun around and galloped up the trail. She watched his white tail disappear among the trees.

Mata sank down on the circular granite rock and prayed to Adi to watch over Caelestis and his herd and all the animals of the valley. She looked up at the ridge they had just descended. The ash was thicker here. Many trees were black. Another faraway rumble. There was no time to ponder. She must find the priestess of the village.

The sharp crack of a branch startled her. Something approached. She had no weapon and didn't think she could run, but she might still be able to make herself seem larger than her physical shell. She imagined herself tall, young, and strong, with the body of a warrior and the stance of an ancient queen.

## Chapter 8

Mata looked down on a slight old man wearing shabby clothing. He stared up at her in wonder. She exhaled back to her normal size.

"That's remarkable," he said. "I have heard of those who can alter their shape, but have never seen it performed. You are a priestess of the Lady, are you not?"

"Do I know you?"

"My village was destroyed in the last eruption, leaving only a few alive. Three of us started walking, hoping to find others."

"Did you find them?"

"A boar attacked us in the lowlands. My friends were killed and I thought surely I would die where I had fallen, but then I regained my strength, quite suddenly. Yesterday, I came to the village below. The people welcomed me."

Mata inspected him. He looked like an ordinary villager, yet there was something strange about him. "What caused your wounds to heal?"

"They have not healed completely. But they no longer pain me." He rolled up one sleeve to show her a deep red gash stretching from elbow to wrist. The cut was deep and angry, but without sign of infection. She stepped closer to him. When he raised his head and looked straight at her, his eyes blazed the color of indigo dye.

She blinked and stepped back. Looked again. His eyes were the same dark brown as every other villager. "With such injuries, why do you not rest below?"

He gestured to his pack. "There is little food in the village. I search for berries."

"The villagers did well to welcome you."

"Are you the one who journeyed to the Graylands to reclaim our holy crystal?"

He spoke quietly, as if he were inquiring about her family line as any stranger might. Still, his words alarmed her. Mata drew back and crossed her arms where the crystal was bound. "Who asks my name without giving his own?"

He lifted both hands in a gesture of apology. "I am Itzal. Without family. Forgive an old man for being curious, but your shape shifting was spectacular. It reminded me of a story told in my village—and in all the valley too—of a priestess named Mata who left long ago from this very village on a quest. Some say the demon of the Graylands killed her. Others say she will return with the crystal and open a gate to a new land."

He had said "long ago." Mata thought about the bustling village of two hundred souls she had left. The Graylands ate time, but surely she had not been gone more than a year.

"How many live below?" she asked.

"A few old people. More younger ones. A few couples."

"How many?"

He shrugged. "Thirty, perhaps."

Mata sat on the flat gray stone. Thirty out of more than two hundred. Who lived? Who had perished? "Is a child with golden hair among them?" she asked. "And her mother?"

"Are you the Mata the people remember?"

"I am. But take heed. In my warrior shape, I can snap you in half, old man."

He stepped back. "Your return is a blessing. I want nothing from you. But what child do you think waits for you? You have been gone more than twenty years."

"Twenty?" Her eyes blinked rapidly. "My daughter's child. My daughter Elem. The child Atarah."

"An Atarah lives below. She is the only priestess. But she is full grown." Mata closed her eyes.

"May I sit here with you?" he asked.

She nodded. He un-shouldered his grimy pack and removed a water pouch. She saw no sign of sorcery about him, but she did not like that he had found her just as she had regained one of her sacred places. His strange eyes made her uneasy.

He offered her water. She shook her head, feeling some of the hardness that had kept her moving toward home slip out of her. She wished he would leave.

"I will leave, but you must come with me."

Her head snapped up. He had heard her thoughts. A magician for sure.

*Who are you?* She thundered into his mind.

Itzal flinched. "Just a traveler seeking shelter. I did hear your thoughts just now, but it is the first time such a thing has happened. Perhaps the shock of losing everything has heightened my perceptions. But I assure you I am no sorcerer and no threat."

"Everything is a threat. I warn you, do not try to deter me."

"I would like to help," Itzal said.

"I must talk to Alarah. Can you go to the village and tell her I am here?"

"I can go. But you must come with me. Everyone will welcome you."

The sky rumbled. "The mountain is ready," she said. Slowly, she rose. Her staff supported her on the right and with Itzal on her left, she could walk well enough.

They followed the path she had trod countless times. She imagined that she remembered each turn, every rock and tree. They passed the meadows that had once been filled with sweetberry bushes and now were bare of leaves. Then they came onto the steepest part of the trail that ended where the old orchard and the forest met. It was slow going, but they reached the bottom safely. Itzal guided her to a fallen log.

"Go," she told Itzal. "I must rest here. Tell Atarah to come."

As he started toward the village, Mata lowered herself to the ground. The sky was dark and fierce. A wind had come up, swirling bits of leaves and ash around her like the slow eddies of a river current. The golden crystal at her waist hummed. She forgot Itzal.

The sound of voices woke her. She grasped the trunk of a tree and pulled herself up. Then they were upon her. Two old women. A young woman. Itzal. They stopped at a respectful distance. The oldest of them, a wizened grandmother, stepped forward.

"The newcomer tells us you are Mata, long lost from our village."

Mata cocked her head and squinted. "Is that you, Eta? I remember you from when we climbed this mountain and found the herb of Adi in a place we never revealed. Do you still use that herb in the *saba*?"

The old woman clasped her hand to her mouth. "We thought you dead or worse. Look." She turned to the others. "Mata has returned from the Graylands." She turned back. "Did you find our crystal? Did you bring it?"

The young woman knelt before Mata. "I am Atarah." Tears streamed down her cheeks.

She was no longer a child, but oh, so beautiful, and still tender in the face. She wore a faded green shift that hung to the ground and a gathering bag across her shoulder. When Mata nodded and extended her hand, Atarah bowed her head. Her hair fell down like a golden curtain.

"I prayed you would come. Since my mother died, I have been alone."

A flash of heat jolted Mata's chest. She embraced Atarah and felt the warm blood coursing through her young veins.

"How did my daughter die?"

"She went with a group to look for food. The mountain exploded while they were gone. The others returned. She did not."

"What of your uncle?"

"No one else is left."

Mata bowed her head. "Have you a priestess?"

"Oh, grandmother. It has always my greatest desire to serve Adi. I was in training, but our priestess died before I could complete my studies. There is no one else. I do my best."

The second old woman stepped forward. "A storm is coming. Let us help you indoors. Then we can talk."

Itzal nodded. He positioned himself on Mata's right. Atarah moved to her left and together they lifted her to her feet.

"I can walk," she protested. They paid no attention and half carried her out of the wood and down the path.

"My house is close," Atarah said.

It was exactly as Mata remembered. The rows of small houses, in evenly spaced curving rows, all facing the round building in the center that contained the *saba* and the temple. The little houses made of mud bricks washed white with lime against the sun and the roofs thatched with the branches of bayberry trees were the same everywhere in the valley, but these were the homes of her friends.

"Does Bec still live there?" She motioned to a house.

"Bec is gone," Atarah said. "And her children. From fever, two years ago."

"These last years have been hard," Eta added. "We thought it would be better if we were all together at the end, so we sent out runners a month ago to see how many are left in the valley. Most have not returned. Itzal joined us just yesterday."

As they passed the rows of houses, Mata saw that each dwelling still had its garden plot outlined with colorful rocks or shells, but nothing grew in them beyond a few weeds. She realized then how many of the houses were deserted.

Atarah's home looked like the others from the outside, but when Mata saw the white stone bench in the empty space that had once been a garden, a wave of memory swept over her. This was the house where she and Sem lived alone after Elem married Ton and started her own household.

Sem had fashioned the bench from a hard stone he found deep in the forest. It looked exactly the same now as the day he finished it. Mata's breath caught as she thought of how many evenings they had sat there and watched the stars.

Mata passed the bench, trailing her fingers along its smooth surface, and went into the house. She sank into a chair by the hearth, again seeing Atarah as a golden baby, how Elem had smiled at her, and how the firelight and the baby had softened the sharp lines of her daughter's mouth. She thought of how Elem had looked like Sem, with her long thin face and deep set eyes. She had never been beautiful, but after the baby came, she had filled out.

Oh my daughter. Forgive me for leaving you.

Atarah filled the teakettle and put plates on the wooden table. Itzal brought two thick logs that caused the flames to jump and crackle. The warmth of the cozy room brought tears to Mata's eyes.

Atarah knelt beside her and held her hands. "What can I do for you, grandmother? The tea is coming and there is dried fruit."

Eta appeared with a small bundle wrapped in cloth. She placed it on the table. "A loaf I made from the wild grain that was brought in yesterday. I offer it to Mata who has fulfilled her sacred mission."

Atarah had already found a knife. She cut a slice of the bread for each person and presented it to them.

"With this bread we celebrate the return of our Mata."

In silence, they ate the bread. Then Atarah and Eta brought out the dried fruit and everyone found a place to sit.

When the food was gone, there came a timid knock on the door. Outside stood a group of villagers waiting in the rain to see Mata.

"She is tired," Atarah told them. "Come back later."

"No," Mata said. "It is their right."

Atarah bowed to her grandmother. She motioned for the villagers to enter. They came in two's and three's, kneeling before Mata, kissing her hands, seeking her blessing. Most she did not remember, but when a stooped old woman carrying a walking stick struggled to kneel on the rug, Mata stopped her.

"Kayla? My neighbor who helped me when Elem was born?"

"Yes. Bless you, Mata."

"Is your husband still with you?"

"No longer. But this is Shay." She motioned to a small man who stood behind her. "He takes care of me now."

A small gray man bowed to Mata. "I played with Elem when we were children. Her loss was a great blow. Thank Adi you have returned."

Mata had a word and a touch for each of them. When all the visitors were gone, she nodded. "It's good they came. Now they have seen me and know there is hope. I must speak to you alone, Atarah. I have a message from Lady Adi."

Eta took her leave. Itzal was half out the door when he turned and looked back at Mata. "They love you," he said.

"They are a loving people. It's not their fault this land became hostile. "

He frowned. "No. I see that." He walked out into the softly falling rain and closed the door behind him.

♪♪♪

I tracked the old woman through the forest to this miserable place with hate burning in my chest because she retrieved her crystal and tamed my sea that was my only companion. But now that I have found her, my hatred does not rise. I hunger still, but not for her. This puzzles me. Still, I must do something. How can anyone without fear of me be allowed to live?

I wonder if that is how Gamani feels. But what does it matter? In all the centuries I lived with a treacherous sea, with no companionship save those I would devour, that is how long the mighty god of the Zhitigal has been silent. His last words to me are burned into my memory. They play over and over, like a priest reciting a holy prayer. Just before he turned his back forever, he said, "The priestess of Adi has won the battle. You must suffer the punishment of her goddess, but only the priestess can set you free."

Then he abandoned me to Adi who drove me to the inland sea with her mighty wind. I was helpless in its grasp, but went willingly enough, for I believed she meant to return me to my men. My warriors had fled all the way to the women's camp, but the unholy wind deposited me at the inland sea, then ordinary water.

Her conditions were simple. I would stay in my assigned realm, which contained the sea and a forest on three sides. On the north was the desert over which the fleeing Zhitigal had disappeared. The land that was my prison would keep the remnants of the Zhitigal and the Caheya apart.

In the beginning, the Zhitigal visited me with offerings of food. They told me how they fared in the northland. Since no new leader had been appointed, they fought each other for the privilege of ruling.

After the animals fled their lands, and they started to starve, they brought me human sacrifices. At first, I was disgusted and refused them. But they brought only young succulent females whose scent made me forget I had once been a man. After I succumbed to my urges to devour the captive females, I truly became a cursed being.

The sea turned thick and black. For every despicable act I committed, the waves grew thicker and darker. The sea harbored an intelligence that hunted any prey venturing near its shore. When there was nothing to eat, I raged against Adi, and my rage contracted the sea, turning it to gelatinous liquid. It was reduced to less than half its size and could no longer be called water, but it was a faithful servant to me until the old woman forced it to stillness. My prison served Adi's purpose, to keep her precious Caheya safe. Now they are as trapped as I. Unless the crystal is indeed a gate. And if it is, where does it lead?

The fires in me are banked. Still, I am curious about all that has transpired. I feel the stirrings of a desire that cannot be slaked by terrified prey. I wander deep into the forest outside the village and turn my eyes toward Adi.

## Chapter 9

Mata gazed at Atarah and she was so full of love, she could not speak the words in her heart. Atarah smiled and grasped her hands. "We will talk in the new land."

Mata nodded. Atarah was a true priestess. "Now we must perform our duties as Adi instructed." She reached inside her tattered shirt and brought out the lump of rag that concealed the crystal. It had congealed into a gray mass.

Atarah reached for the knife still lying on the table.

Mata waited while Atarah carefully cut through the layers of cloth, finally laying open the last covering. When the crystal was free, Mata swept away the cloth and placed the crystal on the table between them. It sparkled as if it had never been wrapped in filthy rags.

"Look at its beauty, Atarah. Truly it is the great healer of our people." The crystal hummed louder when she spoke, its perfectly round shape visibly vibrating. "It is just as the legends say. The crystal contains a gate."

Atarah moved a hand closer to the shimmering golden object. "What will happen?"

"The Lady told me that a priestess must say her holy words over it. You must take it to the *saba* and say the words that Lady Adi gave me while the people pray with you."

Atarah pulled back. "I cannot. I am not a true priestess. My teacher did not know all the rituals and I did not learn all she knew. You must speak the words."

Mata looked at Atarah's lovely face, now wrinkled with worry. "You are the only priestess in the village. I was required to get it back, but you are to speak. Come closer. I will say them to you."

"I am not ready," Atarah protested.

Mata grasped her granddaughter's arm and squeezed hard. "We are all capable of doing our duty. Now listen. The words must be spoken exactly like this."

Atarah leaned closer. The girl's breathing was ragged. She looked terrified, but all that mattered was giving her the words. Mata closed her eyes. Again, she heard Adi's voice speaking the words as she showed them to her in her inner vision. They had been written across the sky with the purest of white clouds.

"Say these words in the midst of the people while the fire burns in the *saba*. Say them with your hands touching the crystal. Say them in your heart before you say them aloud. When you voice them, do so with all your strength. Say them twelve times and then stop."

Atarah nodded.

Mata felt the words inside her quivering with excitement. She took a deep breath. Then she brought forth the words that every High Priestess of the Caheya had spoken in a holy place before she led her people to a new land.

When she finished, she leaned back and closed her eyes. "Go, Atarah. All the people must go to the *saba*. Show them the crystal and tell them to raise their voices in prayer. Go quickly and may Her love give you strength."

Atarah rose. "Come with me. Your voice will give me strength."

"I will watch from Sem's bench."

The door opened. Itzal stood in the doorway. Atarah motioned him to come in. "I must go. Can you help Mata to the *saba*?"

He started to speak, but Mata stopped him with a gesture. "Don't question me. I have completed my task. I will stay here."

"Go, Atarah," Itzal said. "I will stay with her."

"It's not right to leave her here."

"Go now!"

Atarah ran out the door, clasping the golden crystal to her breast.

Itzal stood beside Mata. "She is strong. She will succeed."

Mata thought of Sem who had loved her, of Elem who had waited so long for a child, of Lady Adi who would welcome her home. When Itzal offered her his arm, she allowed him to help her outside. Together, they sat on Sem's bench in the twilight as the people came out of their homes and walked toward the *saba*.

Night fell. The only light was the fire in the *saba*, shining through narrow slits in the mud brick walls. If Atarah succeeded, the gate of Adi would open and a wondrous bridge would form, arching into the next world where the Caheya would be safe.

It was just as they had arrived here so many generations ago. The Lady had shown her an image of the bridge that had brought the Caheya to this valley. It had dazzled Mata with its mass of colored lights strong enough to hold a multitude.

"Will we see it from here?" Itzal asked.

"If she succeeds."

"Has she said the words yet?"

"She has started."

Mata stared at the glimmers of fire. The clouds had parted. Stars hung overhead. She remembered, as a child, being convinced that she could reach them with her hands if she could only climb a high enough hill. If the sacred mountain were not preparing for the final explosion, she could climb to its peak and touch the nearest star. She located it in the north, the bright one that heralded the end of winter.

"Look!" Itzal jumped up. "She has done it."

Mata struggled to her feet. Sparks of turquoise light were shooting out of the *saba*, straight up in the air. Soon they were joined by bright pink lights, then red, green, and yellow. The colored lights coalesced into a pathway of color that vibrated itself into the shape of a bridge that rose higher as it grew longer. It moved northward, with no visible means of support, a span of bright color in the deep night, glowing with life.

"She has done it," Mata whispered. Her eyes blurred. A pain shot through her back and she fell to the ground, landing on both knees. "Stay away," she warned Itzal when he jumped up to help her. "No one touches me without my leave."

"You are a sick old woman," Itzal retorted. "Let me help you to the bridge. It is your creation too."

"Get back." She would allow no sorcerer to touch her during such a holy time.

"Is it better to die keeping the old rules when a new land beckons?"

Mata pulled herself onto the bench and faced Itzal. "You are a mind-reading sorcerer and I will have none of you."

Already the bridge's northern end was out of sight, arching away into the velvet blackness.

"It holds," he said. "The people are coming out of the *saba*. The bridge is beautiful, Mata. I have never seen such a thing."

Thunder clapped. Mata looked up. The stars still shone. "The mountain is ready. They must go now."

"Someone is starting across," he reported. "Can you see?"

"No." Mata murmured. "Tell me."

"A person is on the bridge. Standing up. Moving forward. Another person is climbing up. They are walking across."

Mata inched forward until she was standing next to Itzal. As she watched the two figures moving along the shining path, she felt her heart flowing with pride for Atarah.

Then something happened. The bridge swayed. The people fell. The bridge of light blinked off. Itzal turned to her, his eyes wide.

Mata stared at the bridge. It had disappeared as if it had never been. Then it reappeared, not solid, but blinking in the darkness. The people did not reappear.

"Perhaps the words weren't right," Mata murmured.

"You said the bridge wouldn't appear at all if the words were said incorrectly."

"No one has done this for generations. I have no answers."

Frightened voices called to each other. The people were running from the bridge. Mata imagined them pointing at her, blaming her. She had followed her instructions perfectly, and she believed that Atarah had also been impeccable.

She turned. Itzal's eyes blazed. They smoldered like an indigo sky.

He picked up a rock from the ground and threw it down so violently it made a hole in the rain-soaked dirt. "Can you not that see the bridge needs support? You are high priestess and I am not without power. It is not too late."

Mata turned away. How could she accept help from this decrepit sorcerer? "I have done all that was asked. The Lady must be displeased with me."

"You're a fool, priestess. Are you so blinded by the past you cannot see that something new is needed?"

"How dare you!"

"It's too late to argue. We must help them. Or all will be lost. We can try to balance the bridge. Please, Mata."

Mata thought of the people waiting in the villages of the valley, and the animals in the forest. She saw again the antelope whose life she had spared, and the squirrels who had fed her, and the horse Caelestis. "What shall we do?"

He extended his brown hand toward her. "I feel Adi. I feel her forgiveness. Together we might make enough magic to support the bridge. Come with me. You don't have to cross if you choose death over life, but give the others a chance."

Mata looked at his outstretched hand. She imagined herself reaching for it. She heard the cries of the people as another roar shook the ground.

*What shall I do, Lady? Help me, please.*

A fierce pain stabbed her chest. She gasped. The pain coalesced to a single point like a sharpened dagger piercing her center. Something inside her opened. Warmth gushed out. I am dying, she thought. It felt so warm. The warmth spread through her chest, into her belly, down her arms. Her left hand was on fire. She looked at it and was shocked to see she was clutching Itzal's hand.

He was shouting at her, but she could not hear his words above the rumbling of the mountain. He pulled at her. She took a step toward him, and then they were making their way down the path toward the *saba*. Her legs were stronger. She knew now what she had to do.

The people gathered in a crowd around the *saba*. Atarah broke away and ran to them. "Thank Goddess you've come. The bridge doesn't hold. Two were lost."

"I saw," Mata said. "It's not your fault. Something new is needed. Itzal and I will steady the bridge. When I signal, tell the people to begin crossing. They must not go alone. That was the mistake. They must go in pairs or groups, all holding onto each other."

"I understand." Atarah ran back to the people.

"Come, Itzal. We will stand on opposite sides."

She led him toward the flickering lights that did not seem to be a bridge at all, but a mass of swirling light. Blue dominated the outer edges. Under the darkest blue portion, at the very edge on the western side, Mata positioned herself. She motioned to Itzal to cross under it and stand opposite her.

When they were both in place, she nodded. Together, they raised their arms. As soon as her hands touched the deep blue electric light, the heat of a thousand flames coursed through her body. She couldn't see Itzal, but she knew he was making the same motion. When the blue energy of the bridge had turned as solid as wood under her hands, she looked for Itzal. He stood opposite, his arms raised above his head.

"My side is solid," he called.

She looked down the length of the bridge and saw the solidity spreading along its underside. It was becoming a real bridge, just as Adi had shown her.

Now Mata could perceive farther than her physical eyes could see. The bridge stretched across the entire valley. It wound around each village and stretched through the mountains of the Living Forest. Ramps of light appeared. The people in the villages and the forest animals waited at the ramps for the signal to move onto the bridge.

"It is time."

Over her shoulder she shouted to Atarah, "The bridge will hold. Let the people start across. In pairs and groups. All connected. They must hold onto each other."

"Listen," Atarah called above the thundering of the mountain. "Hold on to someone. Hold hands. Then it will be safe to cross."

Mata heard the footsteps of the first couple move onto the bridge to her right. They blessed her name as they passed above her.

"Tell the others it is safe," Mata called. "And the animals too. The bridge is for all."

"We will tell them," the first couple said. "Mata, from here the bridge is a rainbow, blue on the edges and all colors in the middle, like a great braid. It is so beautiful."

Their footsteps faded. The next group came. They also shouted their thanks to Mata and Itzal for making the bridge safe.

Mata looked down. Her feet and legs had dissolved into warm golden light. She laughed. Her work was complete.

"It's done," she called to Itzal just before her upper half dissolved.

The mountain roared.

Footsteps thudded.

Hoof beats echoed.

"It's done," Itzal called back.

He exploded into a shimmering ball of silver light that hung in the charged air for a brief moment, like a flame bright enough to light the whole world, before it bounced under the rainbow bridge toward the sphere of golden light waiting for him there.

∞

# A NOTE FROM
# THE AUTHOR

If you enjoyed this book, please take the time to write a review and tell your friends about it. Not only do I love hearing your thoughts, but your reviews and recommendations help my stories find the readers who will most enjoy them. Click through to the Kindle store now before you forget.

My fantasy trilogy, The Dreamwalkers of Larreta is available on Amazon.

Follow the dreamwalkers from Earth to Larreta as they race the clock to stop the destruction of two worlds by an unknown force and find their own long lost partners who must re-unite to complete their mission.

The Tyro
The Rending
Kalong

Be the first to hear about my new releases. Register for updates at CarolHollandMarch.com. You will receive monthly information about free books, giveaways, resources for writers and articles.

Follow me on twitter @carolhmarch
Check out my FB Author page.
See my author page on Amazon.com and Goodreads.

# ACKNOWLEDGMENTS

*Desert Song* originally appeared in The Colored Lens, Autumn, 2012

*The Call of The Benu* originally appeared in Penumbra, V 3, Issue 5, 2014

*Dreaming In and Out* originally appeared in Dark Visions, Volume 2, 2013

*The Conversation* originally appeared in Aurora Wolf, 2012

*They Followed Me* originally appeared in Stupefying Stories, March, 2014

*Insemination* originally appeared in The Literary Hatchet #6, May, 2013

*La Loba* originally appeared in Songs of the Earth, Latchkey Tales, 2014

*The Girl Who Couldn't Fly* originally appeared in in Luna Station Quarterly, 2013

www.ingramcontent.com/pod-product-compliance
Lightning Source LLC
Chambersburg PA
CBHW021143130626
46554CB00005B/1642